Dear

About three years ago, when I was living in
Irvine, California, I accepted a job at a high-tech
company in San Diego, about one hundred miles
away. I worked twelve hours on my first day, and
for almost three months afterward I never had a
day off. During that time I became a regular at
the local hotels and motels, courtesy of my new
employer. At one point, when I had stayed in
San Diego longer than anticipated, I was stuck
wearing the same outfit for three straight days.
My company generously provided me with its
very own top-of-the-line logo clothing: two
blouses and an oversize sweatshirt.

When the chip finally taped out, the project
team was treated to lunch at a trendy beachfront
restaurant. I hitched a ride back to work with my
boss in his black Lamborghini. And as the world
sped by me, the idea for *Stick Shift* was born.

This is my first book, and I'm thrilled to be a part
of the FLIPSIDE series. I so look forward to writing
many more, because I now have the time—I don't
have that twelve-hours-a-day job anymore, and
just between you and me, I burned the logo
clothing.

Best wishes!

*Mary Leo*

## "This food should not be fed to a dog!" the deep voice growled beside her

It had been a miserable transatlantic flight, and now Mr. Charming Italian—who smelled deliciously of garlic—wanted to complain about his breakfast. He might be gorgeous, but Lucy wished he would just shut up.

Actually, she thought her tiny omelette du jour, filled with some kind of unrecognizable cheeselike substance, was rather tasty.

"How you eat that? It's not food. It's plastic."

Despite herself, Lucy had to answer him. "I think it's wonderful! Best eggs I've ever eaten."

He made a dismissive gesture and called for an attendant.

Lucy continued to enjoy her breakfast, making little yummy sounds as she chewed. Though parts of the omelette were beginning to taste like dishwater, she'd never say so out loud.

"Take this away. I should eat my shoe rather than smell what you call an omelette," he said to the male flight attendant. "Look," he continued as he pulled off his black leather sandal and everyone turned to watch, even Lucy. "My shoe tastes better." He took a bite.

Ironically, part of his sandal came off in his mouth. Lucy couldn't believe her eyes. Mr. Garlic was actually chewing his shoe.

# *Stick Shift*

## Mary Leo

 HARLEQUIN®

TORONTO • NEW YORK • LONDON
AMSTERDAM • PARIS • SYDNEY • HAMBURG
STOCKHOLM • ATHENS • TOKYO • MILAN • MADRID
PRAGUE • WARSAW • BUDAPEST • AUCKLAND

ISBN 0-373-44181-9

STICK SHIFT

Copyright © 2004 by Mary Leo.

This edition published by arrangement with Harlequin Books S.A.

® and TM are trademarks of the publisher. Trademarks indicated with
® are registered in the United States Patent and Trademark Office, the
Canadian Trade Marks Office and in other countries.

Visit us at www.eHarlequin.com

**Printed in U.S.A.**

## ABOUT THE AUTHOR

*Stick Shift* is Mary Leo's debut novel. She's had careers as a salesgirl in Chicago, a cocktail waitress and keno runner in Las Vegas, a bartender in Silicon Valley and a production assistant in Hollywood. She has recently given up her career as an IC layout engineer to pursue her constant passion: writing romance.

Mary now lives in Pennsylvania with her husband and new puppy.

To my provocative husband,
my three incredible children,
RWASD, WA, Kathryn Lye, Janet Wellington
and the hardworking women in electronics

# 1

LOVE WAS highly overrated, Lucy Mastronardo thought as she yawned and set her alarm clock for 5:00 a.m. All that spooning and mooning crap was for romance novels and love songs, not for real life.

She had always dreamed of the logical mate: a man who had the same goals as she did, a man who found happiness in schedule and conformity, a man who planned out every detail of his life, *their* life, a man who happily sent her off to another continent a week before their wedding because it was "good for your career."

Yes, she could sleep quite soundly knowing that computers made the world go round, not love.

BY THE TIME Lucy awoke at six, having managed to sleep right through the alarm clock's annoying buzz, she was already running late.

The drive on Interstate 280 out of San Jose, California was not what she had expected. Normally, on a Sunday morning it was an empty freeway, but there had been two minor accidents, turning the quick forty-five-minute jaunt into a tedious hour-and-a-half drive.

Then, as if that wasn't frustrating enough, she needed to call her mother to tell her where she was going and why. But the thought of talking to her mother while she tried to maneuver a crowded freeway gave her an immediate stomachache. She decided to put the call off until later, way later, when she was stationary and had some control over her emotions. If she phoned now, she would probably end up causing accident number three and totally miss her flight. Definitely not an option.

Parking at San Francisco airport should have been a snap, but, of course, she had to circle and circle and circle the lot some more, driving up one aisle and down another, until she ended up following a middle-aged man and his white standard-sized poodle through the maze of cars as though she was on stalking detail for the FBI.

When the poodle-man finally found his vehicle, he messed around inside playing with his dog until Lucy was ready to get out and slug him.

Finally, she tapped her horn.

He turned around to look at her.

The poodle turned around to look at her.

They both gave her the evil eye before he drove away.

Fine, she thought, I'm starting my trip out with a curse from a guy and his dog.

The scene inside the airport wasn't any better. From the moment she rolled her suitcase onto the speckled high-grade linoleum, it had been a test of will. Long lines choked the airport, turning the whole travel experience into a nightmare journey.

Fortunately, Alitalia's line seemed to be shorter than the others, which was a good thing, considering she had less than an hour to board her flight to Rome.

While she stood in line with the hundreds of other harried souls in the crowded airport, trifling with the prospect of making that phone call to her mother, and once again deciding to do it later, a young girl in some kind of blue uniform handed out cookies from a silver tray. Like a cookie was somehow going to sooth nerves and make the wait a more pleasurable experience. On the other hand, Lucy mused, if cookie-girl were handing out day-long passes to a spa or vouchers for free housekeeping, now that would most definitely turn this wait into something worth waiting for.

Silly thoughts made the time pass quickly and after Lucy got her prized boarding pass, she had to sprint to the gate, nearly knocking down a few people along the way, until she caught up to a guy who stood in front of her on the moving walkway. He wouldn't step to the right so she could get around him. An annoying guy, with a Giorgio Armani black suede jacket slung over his shoulder, carrying a totally "now" Louis Vuitton brown bag, wearing obviously Italian sandals. The man was an ad for high fashion, who remained ahead of her right before the X-ray line.

He took forever to put his things up on the conveyor belt, as if each item were something sacred, something precious.

Lucy thought about going to the other line, but it was even longer. She wondered why she had hesitated. Why she had stayed to watch when she was in such a hurry. She drew in a deep breath while leaning slightly forward and immediately knew the answer. It was his scent of garlic, not the kind that repelled, but the fresh kind. The aroma that permeates the air when you cut into a really sweet clove.

He went to the tray and removed a small ladle from his shirt pocket, a few dollar bills from another, a garlic press and a head of garlic from his jacket. The security guard immediately confiscated the garlic press.

Lucy stood right next to him while he emptied his

pants pockets of change, car keys, a silver money-clip, a clump of fresh basil and a handful of pistachios.

After he finally walked through without a beep or a buzz, and the guards were satisfied that a garlic press couldn't be used as a weapon, he stuffed everything back into his pockets, one item at a time. She never got a good look at him because he never quite turned around, but it didn't matter. It was the familiar scent that had lured her—garlic, the scent of romantic dinners and passionate love.

Seth, her fiancé and soon-to-be husband, was allergic to garlic. It gave him diarrhea and cramps.

Frustrated with the whole spice adventure, Lucy flew past Garlic Man without so much as a question from the guards or a beep from the metal detector; she had been very careful packing.

Suddenly, there was less than ten minutes to catch her flight. If it hadn't been for Mr. Garlic's scent, and the fact that he looked oh-so-sweet from behind, she would have pushed him aside and yelled out her annoyance. Garlic mixed with a little basil were foods she had learned to live without. Like onions, all they did was give you bad breath and indigestion. But for a moment, a twinkle in time, she had enjoyed the ambiance.

She ran the rest of the way. Fortunately, the boarding gate wasn't very far. Her momentary foolishness about a common herb had almost cost her the flight. She and someone running up behind her were the last two people to board the plane.

Lucy found her row and sat next to the window. Just as she secured her seatbelt and let out an I-made-it sigh, the Italian Garlic Show walked up, boarding pass in hand.

Before she had time to react to the amazing coincidence he said, *"Scusi, signorina,* but you are in my seat."

She turned. "I don't think so," Lucy said, annoyed. "I always sit next to the window."

"Yes. It helps from getting nauseous," he said, standing in the aisle, looking down on her.

"No. I don't get sick. I just like the view."

"And what a beautiful view it is," he said, obviously flirting.

She blushed and pulled out her ticket. Sure enough, she was in the wrong seat. "I'm sorry. I just assumed—"

"An easy mistake," he said and just stood there. Waiting.

She waited, thinking he would be the gentleman and tell her to stay where she was.

He didn't.

"Please take your seats," a male flight attendant said.

Mr. Garlic smiled.

Lucy smiled, but no one moved.

"Is there a problem?" the attendant asked.

"No. No problem," Lucy said.

"We'll be taking off shortly. Please be seated," the attendant repeated.

"Certainly," Mr. Garlic said, smiling. But he didn't budge.

Finally, Lucy gave in with a huff. She gathered her belongings and moved out of the row.

*"Grazie,"* he said and climbed into his victory, sliding his bag under the seat in front of him and draping his jacket around his shoulders, then carefully fastening his seatbelt.

When he finally settled down, he turned and threw

Lucy a contented smile, as if he wanted to start up a conversation on the virtues of correct seating or something.

She was so not in the mood for his smiling chatter.

Instead, she decided to ignore him for the rest of the trip. If she wanted to look out of the window she would gaze out of the opposite one. However, there were three rather large people sitting across the aisle from her, entirely blocking any hopes of seeing anything.

Fine, she thought. I'll just work and sleep. I have a lot to do to prepare for my meeting. I don't need a view.

But a curious thing happened once she strapped herself in and the plane shook with its thrust down the runway. Despite her circumstances and the weirdo sitting next to her, instead of apprehension and her usual flight-fright, Lucy felt excitement.

Joy, even.

What was that about? She blamed her lack of appropriate apprehensions on the sleeping pill she'd taken the night before and settled in with the latest copy of *Complete Woman*, turning to the article entitled, "Rule Your World: 10 Ways to Get Control When Life Feels Wacko."

# 2

"THIS FOOD should not be fed to a dog!" the deep voice beside her growled.

It had been a miserable, turbulent flight so far and now Garlic Guy wanted to complain about his breakfast. Lucy wished he would just shut up.

Actually, she thought her tiny omelette du jour, filled with some kind of unrecognizable cheese-like substance, was rather tasty.

She didn't want to even look at him, even give him the slightest indication she recognized his presence, but he poked her in the arm to get her attention.

"How you eat that? It's not food. It's plastic. That's what it is, plastic food."

Despite herself, Lucy had to answer. "I think it's wonderful! Best eggs I've ever eaten."

He made a dismissive gesture, and called for an attendant.

Lucy continued to enjoy her breakfast, making little yummy sounds as she chewed. She had to admit there were parts of the omelette that tasted like dishwater, but she would never say it out loud.

"Take this away. I should eat my shoe rather than smell what you call an omelette," Garlic Guy said to the male flight attendant who stood in the aisle. "Look," he continued as he pulled off his black leather sandal. Everybody around him turned to watch, even

Lucy. "This shoe, my shoe, tastes better." He took a bite.

Ironically, part of his sandal came off in his mouth. Lucy sat there, gawking. The flight attendant, a tall Harry Potter look-alike, stood spellbound, until some kid said, "Gross!"

Lucy couldn't believe her eyes. Mr. Garlic was actually chewing his own shoe.

Disgusting.

Fine, she thought, I'm destined to be tormented by this shoe-eating, garlic-toting idiot. I must have done something bad in a past life, or the current one, and he's my punishment.

VITTORIO had to admit he amazed himself when a piece of leather came off in his mouth. He never actually meant to eat his own shoe, but there it was, sliding around, mixing with saliva, breaking into pieces. The taste was rather interesting, certainly better than the omelette. Would he actually swallow?

But the girl next to him was waiting. Watching. So, he swallowed. And just like that, Vittorio Bandini had eaten a piece of his own shoe.

"It is good," he said, beaming.

"I'll need you to calm down, sir. And if you want to eat your shoe, please wait until the plane has landed," the attendant said as he removed the offending breakfast tray.

Vittorio put his shoe back on his foot, a concession he went along with because the leather had immediately upset his stomach. And if he didn't relax he would vomit all over the pretty, brown-eyed beauty sitting next to him.

She was the type of girl Vittorio was attracted to, the

type of girl who made his heart race; a beautiful, brown-haired Penelope Cruz type. His dream girl. He would not vomit on his dream girl.

He refused to believe it was the leather, the fine Italian leather, that made him sick, so he blamed it on the foul-smelling breakfast instead. The rotten eggs kept him from making a move on the Madonna next to him, not the shoe leather.

Vittorio unstrapped his seatbelt, pushed himself up from his seat, and stepped over the Madonna, squishing her toe as he climbed out.

"So sorry, *signorina*," he mumbled about a dozen times. She shot him a nasty, pained look and he headed up the aisle toward the toilets.

Never again, Vittorio thought as his stomach churned and flipped. Never again would he eat shoe leather, even if it was Italian.

LIMPING UP the aisle, Lucy found another seat a few rows away from the shoe eater. She wondered what the hell was wrong with her? Why was she being so silly? Who makes yummy sounds over airplane food?

She couldn't come up with an answer.

A young kid in the aisle seat concentrating on his electronic game paid absolutely no attention to Lucy as she crawled over him. He was the perfect traveling companion. She could do anything she wanted and he would never notice.

She popped a couple of Tums, tucked her sore foot up next to her butt and detached the phone in the seat ahead, to call Seth.

When he didn't answer, she left a long-winded message about work and obligation and how much she missed him already and not to worry. She would be back in plenty of time for the wedding.

Their wedding...in exactly six days from that very moment. The vision made her smile: a church filled with family and friends, her dad walking her down the aisle, her white dress (the one her mother made her get...the one that looked like an exploded marshmallow, but she wasn't going to dwell on negatives) shimmering in the sunlight that beamed in through the windows and fell on Seth's face...dear Seth...dear, sweet Seth.

Okay, so he wasn't exactly a "dear" or "sweet" kind of guy. He was more the logical Dilbert kind, who was absolutely perfect for her, if she overlooked his funky sex-only-on-Friday-night habit, and the fact that at twenty-seven she had never had an actual orgasm with him or any other guy for that matter, and the fact that he was obsessed with their careers in electronics.

Actually, she thought he was a lot like her dad—also a design engineer, who promoted working long hours and giving up personal time for the job. The dad-clone-thing traits were just what a girl wanted in a fiancé.

Weren't they?

She dialed Seth's cell phone this time, thinking she needed to apologize for last Friday night. She hadn't been in the mood. "But it's Friday. Sexday," Seth had said, almost whining. Like, Saturday was actually Laundryday, and Sunday, Groceryday. Seth had worked out a daily schedule for his life, *their* life, but for some reason, lately, Lucy wasn't able to keep up.

A perky blond flight attendant with a pasted-on smile interrupted the apology-call to offer her a cup of coffee.

Lucy snapped the phone into its holder.

"No, thanks," Lucy said, thinking perhaps she'd make the call later, once she was settled in her room, once she could come up with a logical reason why packing had seemed like a better alternative to Sexday.

The shoe eater stood in the aisle directly behind the attendant, looking rather ill. He wasn't particularly handsome, his nose was a little too long, his hair too shiny-black for his light olive skin, and he had the strangest colored eyes, some sort of a brown-hazel-green combination.

She couldn't imagine what all the fuss had been about. Why she had to move in closer when she stood behind him in line. Why she had to watch him as he ate his shoe, or felt the need to tell him about her breakfast. He was just your typical, ordinary, unexceptional quirky guy.

Then he smiled. Smiled right at her.

A mischievous grin that required a return gesture. It was a natural reaction. A reflex. A totally spontaneous occurrence that gave her goose bumps and made her toes itch. The guy was so utterly charismatic. So completely awesome that she had no choice but to return his beam. With that smile, he looked like the type of guy who could have a hot babe draped on each arm.

Cufflinks, Sinatra used to say.

She smiled right back at him, a wide, toothy Julia Roberts grin.

Don't stare, she told herself as he tried to make his way past the attendant, but Lucy was powerless. There was something about him.

Something in the way he moved.

She noticed his hands first, the long fingers with the manicured nails that grabbed at the backs of the seats for balance as the plane hit a pocket of turbulence. She wondered what they would feel like against her skin—soft and smooth or rough with calluses?

She liked the way his deep-green sweater clung to his trim body. Liked the way it made his skin seem to glisten. She even liked the way he wore his hair, cropped short, almost old-Roman style, but with skinny sideburns.

A great look, she thought. Seductive.

Lucy continued to stare as he walked right past her without a word. Without so much as a nod of recognition, as though he had been smiling at air.

She sighed and turned toward the window. Bright blue. Miles and miles of bright blue. As if the plane wasn't moving at all. As if she were caught in a blue capsule, suspended in the middle of forever. The thought made her stomach roll as she searched inside her purse for a tranquilizer.

As IT TURNED OUT, the shoe leather settled nicely inside Vittorio's stomach and the walk to the toilets cleared away any lingering nausea. Perhaps it wasn't the walk at all, Vittorio thought, but the *bella signorina* staring up at him. The girl he had been sitting next to, wearing a beautiful white pant suit with her shoulders wrapped in a red scarf. Now that he had dared to get a good look at her, he never wanted to look at another. *Que bella!*

He could not leave the airplane without officially meeting her.

By the time he decided to turn around with his new mission, a serving cart blocked any hope he had of meeting the beauty in red.

Attendants busied themselves with morning liquids, forcing him to wait.

Vittorio had come from *Italia* to San Francisco to attend a culinary conference at the Masconi Convention Center. Ever since he was a young boy, he had wanted to see San Francisco. It was only in the last year, when his small restaurant in *Napoli* had become a hit, that he could afford the trip. *La Bella Note* was a huge success due to Vittorio's scrumptious recipes.

The conference had proved to be disappointing for Vittorio. He'd thought he would learn something new, something exciting, but instead he had taught the teachers. One man, who called himself an Italian chef, tried to make a pistachio pesto with nuts that came from North Carolina.

Vittorio didn't exactly know where North Carolina was located in the United States, but he did know it wasn't anywhere near Sicily. Anyone who called himself an Italian chef would know there were no other pistachios in the entire world to compare with the flavor of the Sicilian pistachio. Its silky herbal oil, and its vibrant green color exuded an incomparable flavor experience. Vittorio had brought a bag with him and had remade the pesto sauce for the ricotta ravioli. The chef couldn't believe the difference in taste and invited Vittorio to cook with him on his TV show the next time he came to America.

But it would probably never happen because Vittorio hated to fly. To him, it was like being trapped inside a moving tin can without any room for mingling.

It amazed him that people flew so often they actually accumulated enough miles to fly for free. A car was better, or a ship. At least he could meet people along the way, and meeting people, especially women, was something Vittorio made a career of, like the Madonna sitting alone in the last row of the plane.

"Can you believe this?" he asked the long-legged

blonde reading a Dean Koontz thriller. "I pay all the money and I cannot sit in my own seat."

"Please," she said with a sultry, deep voice. "There are plenty of seats in this row. Be my guest."

Vittorio smiled and sat down right next to his latest dream girl.

WHEN THE PLANE landed in Rome on Monday morning, Lucy let out a sigh of relief. She had been busy on her laptop writing memos and creating charts for work. She had also made up a list of last-minute wedding details she would e-mail her mother later. Now she genuinely looked forward to the three-hour drive to Naples. She would listen to some local music, drink in the atmosphere, and grab a sandwich somewhere along the way because she honestly hadn't been able to eat another airplane omelette.

Lucy actually toyed with the idea of postponing the eleven-thirty meeting with Giovanni, the lead engineer at Subito, the satellite for B-Logic, her Silicon-Valley-based electronics company. What she wanted more than anything else at that precise moment was a hot bath in her sure-to-be-fabulous room at the Santa Maria, but the chip had to tape out in a week to come out of fabrication in time for a demo at the Design Automation Conference in August. B-Logic could not afford to miss the show. Perhaps if she made a beeline to the car-rental counter she could make up some time on the road and get that bath before the meeting. A girl can only hope, she thought.

But she still had one major problem to take care of...her mother. Lucy hadn't had the courage to make the call on Friday afternoon when she'd first found out that her promotion depended on this last-minute trip to Italy. And on Saturday she was busy packing, and she most definitely couldn't call on the freeway and SFO was just too hectic. The real reason she hadn't called was pure terror. Her mother would probably pop a vein over this whole thing, and Lucy wanted to be as far away as possible. She flipped opened her cell phone and pressed 9.

It only rang once.

"It's late. What's wrong?" her mother demanded.

The woman had a sixth sense. "Is that any way to answer your phone?"

"I knew it was you. Something's wrong. My feet are burning."

"It's a hot flash."

"I don't have those anymore. Not since I got on the hormones. My feet only burn when there's something wrong with my daughter."

"Go soak your feet. There's nothing wrong."

"You're not telling me the truth."

Lucy sighed and leaned up against a wall. "Okay, you're right. I'm on my way to Naples for work."

"Now you go to Italy? I could never get you to go to Italy and for work you can go a week before your own wedding?"

"Mom, calm down."

"Where are you?"

"In Rome."

"I knew there was something wrong all night with you. I kept dreaming about garlic. How's what's-his-name taking this?"

"His name is Seth. Shouldn't you try to remember it if he's going to be your son-in-law?"

"It's a hard name to remember."

"It's four letters."

"Not enough. If it were more, I could remember. Four is too few."

"My name has four letters."

"*Lucia* has five. It's better."

"Mom!" Lucy said, exasperated. Her mother had a way of making the simplest things into a major deal.

"You're gonna miss the wedding. Your mother is gonna be ashamed because her only daughter is gonna miss her own wedding. I won't be able to go out in public."

"I'll be back on Friday."

"I know in my heart that you like to shame me, so there I'll be, standing in church, in front of God, with your father in an expensive rented suit, a hundred angry guests and no daughter. I knew when you were born this day would come."

"Mom, I can't talk to you anymore. I have to go."

"Bring back some good prosciutto. I got a taste for some prosciutto from *Napoli*."

"I'll see if I have time."

"Oh, for strangers you have plenty of time, but for your mother *you'll see?*"

"You know, this is why children never call their parents."

"Be safe, and always keep your purse close to you. Those Neapolitans are crooks and thieves."

"Dad's family is from Naples."

"I know what I'm talking about. Tie a bell on your toe in case you sleepwalk."

"The bell never worked. Besides, I don't do that anymore."

"How can you know? You're asleep."

Lucy could feel the agitation building. Could feel the

back of her neck tense until she could barely move it. "All right!" she said. "I'll get a bell."

"Why you want to yell at your mother like that? I'm just trying to keep you from getting hurt."

Lucy sighed again. "I know. I'm sorry."

"Your father wants to say something."

Lucy waited with her eyes closed while they argued over what he was going to say. Her mother kept telling him not to talk too long because this was costing Lucia money. In the meantime, Lucy stood there waiting, calling, "Mom! Just let him talk. Mom!"

Finally, her father got on. "Lucy, honey, have a productive trip. Don't be afraid to show those people who's boss."

She pictured her dad holding on to the phone, her mother standing next to him counting the seconds. Her dad would be wearing his Sunday outfit. He believed in uniforms and wore the same thing every day. The color of the shirt varied, but the pants were always black Dockers, except on casual Friday, then the Dockers would be changed for his one pair of Levi's. "I'll try, Dad."

"That's all anyone needs to succeed, the right attitude and you've got it made. Go get 'em."

Her mother told him, "that's enough," so he said his goodbyes and her mom got back on the phone.

"I want you to look up the Donicos while you're there. I hear the boy is a big shot."

"Mom, I really don't think I'll have any free time."

"Is this how I raised you? To be so selfish to your own mother?"

Lucy gave up. She couldn't argue anymore. "Okay, I'll look up the Donicos. I'll find a bell. I'll keep my purse close, and I'll get the pound of prosciutto. Can I please go now?"

"You should have gone a long time ago. What do you think? I got all night to be on the phone with you? I got things I gotta do for the wedding. I gotta order some nice red carnations for the altar. Love you," she said, kissed the air two times and hung up. Lucy collapsed in a nearby chair.

When she finally regained her composure about fifteen minutes later, she was gliding down the crowded escalator in Leonardo da Vinci airport, spotting Eurocars International and a feeling of accomplishment swept over her. Even with her phone call to her mother, she was ahead of her own schedule.

Then she saw the line of people standing in front of the counter. It was all that secretary's fault at the Italian office. She had made the travel arrangements. Lucy had told the girl that she wanted to fly directly into Naples, but the girl, probably an airhead, couldn't get her on a connecting flight. She could book it on the return, but not on the arrival. So this was the result.

Sigh.

San Francisco and Leonardo da Vinci airports might have different names and be on different continents, but the lines were all the same. Long.

So much for hot baths and sandwiches.

It was a beautiful morning, from what she could see out the huge windows surrounding her, but each person in line had to quibble with the staff behind the counter over silly things like the color of the car, or the quality of the radio or the size of the engine. Lucy thought it was insane. Rome waited a few steps outside these walls and all anybody seemed to care about was the color of paint.

She let out a series of yawns. Her ears crackled, then popped. She could hear again. The crowded airport was unexpectedly loud, and the people in front of her seemed to be setting the pitch.

She had to restrain herself from jumping into the fray, from yelling out her own innocuous frustrations, like a cranky kid unhappy about a purple sucker when she wanted a green one.

Was it something about Italy? About the culture? It seemed as though when a non-Italian arrived, and there were plenty of non-Italians standing in front of her, they suddenly developed the Italian instinct to argue. Your normal, average, calm Brit or Spaniard or Frenchman abruptly found themselves whining over every last detail. Every minute inconvenience. And the irony was, everyone seemed to enjoy the banter. She thought there was something wonderfully liberating about public bickering and no one noticing.

When it was finally her turn, Lucy wheeled her suitcase up to the counter, calmly reached into her purse, took out her driver's license and smiled at the chubby, short woman standing behind the gray counter. "Hello," said Lucy. "I have a reservation for a compact, automatic."

"No automatic. Stick," the woman said as she reached for Lucy's driver's licence and read her name out loud. "*Signorina* Lucia, only stick."

"I can't drive a stick shift. I'm sure the reservation was for an automatic," Lucy replied in a calm, clear voice.

The woman's voice went up an octave. "We no got no automatic. Just stick. You want or not?"

Lucy spoke in Italian. "I want the car I ordered."

The woman responded in Italian, "I'm sorry, miss,

but they're all gone. If you want a car, you'll have to take a stick. That's all I have."

"You're not listening. I can't drive a standard. I *need* an automatic. Surely you can understand—"

"You want a car? I give you a car. So you have to learn something new. So what!"

Lucy hesitated, counted to ten and thought of Sister Gregory; stern, unemotional Sister Gregory from ninth grade. *It's time you learned something new, young lady. Time you learned how to swim.* Lucy remembered the shock as she hit the cold water and the silence as she sank to the bottom of the pool like a schoolhouse desk. The only good memory of that day was Sister Gregory, brown habit and all, jumping in after her.

"Look, I have to drive all the way to Naples and I don't have the faintest idea—"

"I can drive you," someone said in English. It came from behind her. Lucy turned to see none other than Mr. Garlic.

"Not you again," she said, dismissing his offer.

"*Perdona*, but have we met?"

Lucy realized just how rude she must have sounded, and how unimportant she must have been to him because he didn't even remember her. She softened her voice. "No, we haven't actually met. Not officially, but I remember you from the flight. I was in your seat and you ate my shoe...your shoe. You ate your shoe, not mine...I mean."

"Ah, I am famous!" he said, full of himself.

"For fifteen minutes."

He smiled, and once again Lucy felt the heat of his attraction. Her toes itched. She wiggled them inside her shoes, trying to get the itch to stop, but it wouldn't, not as long as he stood in front of her, smiling.

He was taller than she had first thought, at least six feet, but then she had never been this close to him, at least not facing him. And the scent of garlic was gone, replaced now with the scent of basil. How odd, she thought, for someone to smell of herbs.

"Thank you for the offer, but I can drive myself," she said.

"Nobody with a brain wants a car in *Napoli*," he answered.

She didn't like the implication. "You have a car. What does that make you?"

"No brains. My mamma, she always say I got no brains, so I buy a car. Please, allow me to drive you to *Napoli* in my brainless car."

Lucy had to smile at his innocent chivalry.

"You want the car or not, miss?" the woman roared.

Lucy stood unnerved in the midst of airport chaos and tried to decide what to do with his offer. If this were the U.S. and some eccentric guy volunteered a ride, she would absolutely refuse. He could be some crazed killer. But this was Italy.

Her Italy.

Her heritage.

And for the most part, Italian men were romantics, lovers...she noticed the head of garlic sticking out of his shirt pocket.

"Thanks, but I'll be fine," she said thinking this man was some kind of food-kook.

"*Buona fortuna!*" he said and turned abruptly away. She watched as he joined the mix of travelers roaming through the airport. He stopped to wave goodbye as if they were old friends and he was leaving on some trip. She wiggled her toes and caught herself waving back, feeling sad. There was something intoxicating about him, but she couldn't think about that now. There wasn't any time to question her emotions. She'd think about it later, while she was soaking in a hot tub, scrubbing her toes.

For an instant, she regretted never having taken the time to visit Italy, but she was always so busy with work, and before that there was college, then grad school. Not that she didn't love Italy. She did. She loved hearing stories about it, reading about it, learning the language, but she could never justify an actual visit, and yet here she was. Alone. On a business trip. A week before her wedding. At least she could enjoy the scenery from the car, even if she would have to learn how to drive along the way.

"I'll take the car," Lucy told the woman behind the counter.

The woman looked at her and spat, "Sorry, I gave your car away. No more cars."

"What? You must have misunderstood. I'll take the car now."

"All rented. No more cars, miss. Come back tomorrow. I can get you an automatic tomorrow."

"Tomorrow! What do you mean *tomorrow?*" Lucy's voice went up an octave, but she caught herself. She refused to get into a shouting match. "Thank you," she said in a tight, subdued tone. "I'm sure you did your best."

The woman behind the counter didn't reply as Lucy ran off after Mr. Garlic, hoping his offer was still good, when suddenly she realized she didn't know his name.

# 3

THE GIRL in the red scarf had so intrigued Vittorio that once the plane had landed in Rome he followed her to the car-rental counter. Fortunately, they were going to the same city, but the beguiling Madonna had turned out to be an elitist.

Her misfortune, Vittorio thought as he waved his goodbye. He was not the type of man to pursue a woman with her nose stuck up in the air when there were so many unspoiled women to choose from, like the girl serving him the cappuccino from behind the coffee bar. The girl with the beautiful, full breasts and round hips who leaned toward him just enough so he could peek down her open blouse.

"Just right," Vittorio told her as she moved in even closer, smiling over at him when she put the cup, with the billows of steamed milk, down in front of him. "Like a pillow," he teased and picked up the cup to take a sip. She giggled and her breasts bounced ever so slightly under the thin cotton of her floral blouse.

Vittorio appreciated the moment and was just about to start some heavy flirting when somebody tapped him on the shoulder.

"Excuse me," a voice said, tap-tap-tapping while he tried desperately to get his peek at what had to be the most perfect breasts in all of Italy.

"Go away. I am busy," he said as he turned around, annoyed by the incessant pecking on his shoulder.

It was she, the elitist in the red scarf. Her hair had come undone from its clip and surrounded her face with its rich luster. Streaks of sunlight sparkled through the warm brown of thick silk.

Vittorio could only smile at his fortune. To be enveloped by two such beauties was indeed a great moment to be savored.

"Ah, it is you, *signorina*. Let me buy you a cappuccino," he said, smiling.

"Thanks," Lucy said, "but I thought you were driving to *Napoli*."

"Yes, but first I drink coffee. Please, you will feel better after." He turned to the beauty leaning on the counter. *"Prego, un cappuccino."*

Lucy hesitated, but then agreed, rolled her suitcase in close, and secured her purse on her shoulder. The girl behind the counter continued to flirt with Vittorio as she made the cappuccino for Lucy.

The girl and Vittorio spoke to each other in Italian.

"Is this your lover?" she asked Vittorio.

"What kind of question—"

"Just making sure," she said.

When she had finished making the cappuccino, she slammed it down in front of Lucy, spilling the coffee on the counter and on Lucy's white jacket.

"Thanks a lot," Lucy said and reached for a napkin.

Undaunted, the girl walked back to Vittorio and leaned in as far as she could. This time Vittorio got the full view.

"Oh, brother," Lucy murmured and turned away.

"I get off work in an hour," the girl purred.

"Don't let me stop you," Lucy said, as she picked up her things and walked away.

Vittorio called after her. "No. Wait." He pulled some money out of his pocket, put it down on the counter, smiled and whispered, "Some other time, perhaps."

"Some other time," the coffee girl repeated, with fire in her eyes.

LUCY COULDN'T BELIEVE she had decided to hitch a ride from such a...a lush, a sleaze, a guy with absolutely no scruples. To flirt with one girl, while another waits for you, was just...well, it was disgusting. Downright disgusting!

But then it was the nature of the Italian man to flirt. Her very own father was a flirt. Somehow, her mother never cared. She would say, "Better that he looks at the menu than eat the food."

Disgusting!

If the earth opened up at that very moment and swallowed the whole group of them, she would be happy. Jubilant! Filled with jubil.

As she walked through the airport, pondering her new descriptive phrase, envisioning a huge crack down the middle of Italy where thousands of smirking Italian men, dressed in trendy suits and black sandals lined up to jump into the abyss, she felt a tap, tap, tap on her shoulder and turned.

"*Scusi, signorina.* Please, my car, she waits," he said, bowing.

Lucy stood there, staring at him while she did a mental rewind of the smile they'd exchanged on the plane.

"Then, let's go," she said.

He slung his bag over his shoulder and reached for

her suitcase, but her stubborn streak wouldn't let her give it up.

"Please," he said. "Allow me."

"Thanks, but I'm perfectly able to pull my own bag."

He looked at her, puzzled. "But why, when I am willing to pull it for you?"

She couldn't think of a quick response, so she gave him the suitcase, but it somehow didn't seem right. She walked alongside him with her arms folded across her chest. Lucy believed in equality, women's rights, NOW, and didn't particularly like it when a man showed any degree of old-world chivalry. She wanted to give him a lecture on how things were in her world, but decided this was his world so she would let it go...for now.

They walked for what seemed like forever. After hopping on at least three trams, they finally found his car in the multi-story carpark. It was a bright-red, classic, convertible Alfa Romeo Spider about the size of a tight shoe.

Lucy wondered where inside this tiny flash on wheels was the luggage going to fit. He opened her door, of course, making sure she was comfortable before he crammed the luggage into the itty-bitty trunk.

When he got in and shut his door, Lucy realized just how close they were. She could actually hear him breathing.

Help!

Suddenly, she thought of Seth. Longed for Seth. Longed for his arms around her. His face next to hers. His body so close they were one. To be cuddling with him as they watched an old movie, or lingered over a spectacular sunset—even though they'd never watched an old movie or lingered over a sunset, she was sure they would once they were married.

"I've got to make a phone call," she blurted and jumped out of the car. She didn't care that Seth was on his workday-sleeping schedule and was probably tucked in for the night. She only cared about one thing...hearing his reassuring voice.

At first she couldn't get through, then Seth's phone began to ring.

"Hello," he said into her ear. It felt great to hear his voice. Made her think everything was going to be fine. That this trip was worth the effort.

"Hi, Seth. Just wanted to tell you that I'm here," she told him.

Just at that moment, the red sportscar roared to life. "I can't hear you. You'll have to shout," Seth said. "Where are you?"

"In Rome."

"I thought you were going to Naples."

"I'm driving. Well, I'm not driving but...I met someone who—"

"You're breaking up. All I got was something about you...meeting someone."

"What? I can barely hear you." She tried to shout louder over the revving engine, but the noise only grew worse.

She thought she could hear Seth as he yawned into the phone. "Everything's under control here, so don't worry. Just concentrate on work. Your mother phoned. She's taking over the wedding. Ordering more flowers. Carnations. Red ones." He yawned again. "Call me when you get to your room."

"But *you* were supposed to handle all the last-minute

stuff for me, not my mother. She'll turn it into an Italian festival. I hate red carnations!"

"Don't worry so much. It'll be fine. I have to go to sleep now, or I won't get my eight hours. You know I'm lousy without my eight."

"Seth, I—"

"Bye," he said before she could get another word out. Before she had a chance to tell him she loved him. Before he could tell her he loved her. Not that they had said it very often, twice to be exact, twice in the year and a half they had been dating, but it was an overused word anyway.

Wasn't it?

The phone went dead.

For an instant Lucy thought she should call him back. Tell him it was some guy she met on the plane, some weird guy who eats his shoes and smells of garlic. She was getting a ride from a complete stranger who had an unhealthy fascination with garlic and leather. Someone who carries her luggage, opens her car door and flirts with every woman he sees.

Someone who makes her toes itch.

She wanted to tell Seth everything, wanted him to get angry, jealous, enraged, but instead she opened the car door and slid into the seat next to...oh my God, she still didn't know his name.

# 4

"THE FASTEST WAY to Naples is the *Autostrada del Sole*," Lucy ordered even before she closed her door, as if he were a taxi driver and she were the passenger. She was staring at her glossy map that she had purchased at Barnes and Noble the minute she found out she would be going to Italy. "You can drop me off at the Santa Maria. Do you know where that is?"

"Yes," he calmly said. "A beautiful hotel."

"And don't get any ideas. I'm getting married on Saturday."

"This Saturday?" he asked.

"Yes, this Saturday. Is there something wrong with Saturday?"

"No. What could be wrong? If you say you're getting married on Saturday, then you're getting married."

"On Saturday," she repeated.

"This Saturday," he said, but there was something in his voice that drove her nuts. Some bit of sarcasm or skepticism that made her want to scream. She folded her arms across her chest.

They were silent as he backed the car out of the parking spot. The quiet made her tense. Agitated. She felt as if he were judging her.

"It's not like it's a big wedding. Just a hundred or so people. My fiancé is handling everything. And my mother is ordering more flowers, a girl can never have too many flowers...red carnations. I love red carnations."

Okay, so she lied, but she was going for some kind of response here. She didn't exactly know why, but she wanted a response.

Still nothing.

He drove the car around the parking lot, squealing through the turns, then slowing on the next guy's bumper. He drove like a maniac.

Nutso.

He finally said, "I got to make a couple stops. We take *Appia*, you will like it better. I am Vittorio, Vittorio Bandini."

"Lucy Mastronardo," she told him, tensing as he hit the brakes, almost hitting the yellow Mini in front of them.

He turned to look at her. "Then, you are Italian!"

"Only by blood. I was born in America," she said.

"You don't like your blood?"

"No...yes. It's fine blood. What I mean is, I'm marrying an American."

"That's nice, but you will still be Italian."

"You don't understand."

"Perhaps, but you cannot change who you are by marrying someone you are not."

She stared at him for a moment, then at her map and said, "The *Appia* will take too long. I can't afford the time."

"Lucia, this is *Italia* and you are Italian. All you got is time." He shifted gears and drove the car out into the morning sun.

Lucy could never understand the fascination men had with a stick shift, all that movement, up and down, back and forth. It seemed like such a waste of energy and time. Such a dated way to drive a car. Maybe you had to have a penis to understand the connection.

"I have to attend a meeting at a company," she told him while fastening her seatbelt. She had to admit that the interior of the car was lush and comfortable compared to her Camry. This whole thing was beginning to get to her. She folded her map and shoved it into her brown Coach purse.

"Ah, Lucia, you think they care if you are late? If you stop to enjoy the ambiance of *Italia*? No. I do not think so. Maybe in America you must not be late, but Americans are silly people. They work too much. Can't enjoy life."

"Isn't there a train I can take? Maybe you should drop me off at a train station."

"Sure. There are trains, but why take a train when you can take me?" he said, smiling. "I am better than a train. No?"

Okay, so he's better than a train, she thought. Better than almost anything, with that candy-talk and enticing smile, but she came to Italy for work, not play. And, she was getting married on Saturday.

This Saturday.

She took out her phone and called Subito. No one answered. She hung up and dialed again, thinking she had pressed the wrong number. Still no answer. She didn't understand. The project had to go out in a week. There were customers and demos, and money to be made. They should be practically living at work, sleeping under their desks on futons, showering only when absolutely necessary and ordering in.

As Vittorio drove away from the airport, he said, "See, I was right. You should listen to me, Lucia."

Lucy left a message for Giovanni, excusing herself

for missing the morning meeting. Then she ordered a mandatory meeting for the entire team at one o'clock sharp, thinking that would give her plenty of time to arrive. She wanted everyone to be ready for a "show-and-tell," complete with pen plots, schematics, and simulation results for every block on the communications chip. "Plan on an all-nighter," she said into the phone. "Have your secretary order a couple pizzas."

She snapped shut her phone and sank into the comfortable seat and tried to enjoy the view—the countryside, not Vittorio.

Once they were on the road to Naples, Lucy relaxed and let her mind wander to what she had learned about Italy, her Italy. As they drove, windows down, wind caressing her body, she knew she was finally home.

The view was spectacular, more breathtaking than she had ever thought it could be—the expanse of sea to her right and the terraced hills to her left. The air, clean and sweet.

Lucy's mother had wanted to return to Italy several times, but her dad always came up with an excuse why they shouldn't. Besides, high-school summers needed to be spent taking extra classes, preparing for college.

Her dad, who was a third-generation Italian and had no bond to Europe, had taught her about getting ahead in the world, about working hard for what you wanted, and about keeping one's voice at a calm, low pitch.

"Lucia," Vittorio said. "You like *Italia?*"

She nodded. "I've heard a lot about it. My mother's from Positano."

"*Que bella!* A beautiful town by the sea. And your mamma, her family, they still live in Positano?"

"No. When my grandparents died everyone moved away. I guess I'd like to see it someday."

"You want, we can go. Positano is no far from *Napoli*. I know where to buy homemade Limoncello. The best!"

Lucy didn't like his intrusion into her personal life, as if he had some kind of right because they were both Italian.

"No, thanks," she said, trying to dismiss the conversation, but his words kept nagging at her, making her feel guilty, the way her mother always did. She didn't have time to visit ancient villages. She had a chip to get out. Maybe some other visit, like for her first wedding anniversary. Maybe then, she and Seth would come back for a real honeymoon since there was no time for one now. They had planned a weekend in San Francisco, but Monday morning was work as usual. They were both on hot projects.

Perfect, she thought. She would return to Italy for their first anniversary and visit her mom's hometown.

Definitely maybe, if there wasn't a project in the way.

"Then, why are you here?"

"For business," she said, and sat upright in the seat, hoping he would get the body language and turn off the fountain of questions.

"You make lots of money in this business?"

She shot him a look, then realized it was just an innocent question.

"I'm comfortable," she looked over at him as he drove, shifting gears to slow down behind a bus, then shifting again to speed up to get around. It looked easy enough. She thought she probably should have taken the rental car right off. She just had a momentary panic, that's all. She wouldn't let it happen again.

"You no look so comfortable. You look, how you say? Tense," he said, looking over at her.

"It was a long flight," she mumbled.

Vittorio drove the car off an exit. Lucy asked, "Why are we getting off? We still have a long way to go."

"We are in Frascati. The white wine is like nowhere else in *Italia*. *Delizioso!*" he drew his fingers together and kissed them. Lucy hadn't seen that gesture for so long she had forgotten all about it. And there it was again. Vittorio had a way of making it look sultry, sexy, as if he were kissing a woman's lips. "Sweet and exciting," he said.

"I bet," Lucy answered, smiling in spite of herself.

He parked his car behind a row of colorful stucco buildings: green, yellow, pink and blue. He walked over to her side of the car and opened the door before she had time to unfasten her seatbelt.

"Thank you, but I can get my own door," she told him. He dismissed her comment.

Lucy stepped out of the car onto the cobblestone street and felt as if she had been swept away in a fairytale. At once she could hear the village as it came to life around her. She didn't know how anyone might have ignored the sounds of Italy.

As she stood up and looked out over the hills behind the car, she could see the steeples and rooftops of Rome and the dome of Saint Peter's Cathedral. The ancient city had a pink glow all its own. The vast expanse of architectural and artistic masterpieces took her breath away and brought a momentary rush of excitement.

"*Magnifico*, no?" Vittorio said, as he gazed at the unbelievable view.

"Yes," was all Lucy could manage to say as she turned away from the spectacle of Rome and walked toward the colorful buildings of Frascati, a village she had never heard of.

"You will feel better after a little wine, some bread, a little prosciutto."

"I can't drink this early in the day."

"There is no right time for wine. Wine keeps your blood flowing."

"My blood flows just fine, thank you."

"A small glass of wine and a little food, perhaps," he said, tilting his head, smiling at her.

She caved. "Okay. Maybe a tiny glass, but only because my internal clock is messed up anyway. But I'm not the least bit hungry," she said, lying, wishing again she had rented the stick shift when it was first offered, thinking that by now she would have mastered the damn thing and been halfway to Naples, alone, thinking about work rather than a Roman holiday.

"Whatever you want," he said, smiling.

Sigh.

Vittorio came up behind her and guided her through the back door of Cantina Fienza, a dark, musky-smelling winery with three walls covered in wine barrels stacked on wooden shelves. There were a few small tables clustered in the center of the room, and wine-making tools littered the floor. The ceiling, a fresco, depicted naked men and round naked women clutching bunches of purple grapes in evocative positions. She wondered if the artist had used live models.

For some reason, Lucy blushed.

A short, roly-poly man came toward them, smiling.

He yelled out Vittorio's name with his arms outstretched and a look of delight on his deeply tanned face.

They hugged and kissed each other's cheeks and spoke in Italian. "Vittorio, my nephew, it's been a long time," the man said as he stepped back from him.

"Ah, Antonio, it's good to see you," Vittorio answered.

"And who is this beautiful woman?" Antonio asked.

Vittorio spoke in English. "This is Lucia. My friend."

Antonio leaned in and hugged Lucy. Her tiny body pressed up against his soft chest. For an instant, she felt safe, warm, welcomed, but the moment passed and she pulled away. She was getting far too sentimental.

"Come, sit down and taste my wine," he said.

She followed his directions and sat at a small, round table with Vittorio. There were a few other people in the cantina, drinking espresso mostly, laughing and talking with such enthusiasm that it seemed as if the place were crowded, but it wasn't. Most of the tables were empty.

Soon there were several glasses in front of them filled with different shades of white wine, an assortment of cold meats, cheese and olives.

"First, you try the golden wine." Vittorio slid a glass toward her. "It cleans the tongue."

Lucy was a little hesitant thinking about the tranquilizer she had taken. Vittorio insisted. She took a sip—a musky-tasting wine, dry, with an almond aftertaste.

She liked it and took another drink, a big one.

"*Perfecto*, no?" Vittorio beamed. He handed her a slice of prosciutto wrapped around a piece of melon. She took a bite. Totally terrific.

"*Perfecto!* Yes," she declared, beaming.

Somewhere, music played, mixed with laughter. Lucy liked the way the place made her feel. Festive, she thought as she wrapped her red Chanel scarf around her shoulders.

Next, she tried the more yellow wine, crisp, clean, the kind of wine that warmed the palate. She tore off a chunk of bread and ate a few green olives.

"Have some cheese. It's good for you. Makes your bones strong," Vittorio said, cutting off a chunk big enough for a family of four. But it was wickedly creamy and melted in her mouth.

More wine. She needed more wine.

"I really shouldn't," she said after she downed another glass. When they'd finished off the two white wines, she decided to try the blush. It was sweet, a little floral tasting and went down easily along with the cappocolo, one of her favorite Italian sliced meats. She carefully folded each tender slice inside a crust of bread, spread open a couple olives and removed the pits, then placed the olives on top of the meat, then a drizzle of olive oil, a thick slice of cheese, another gulp of wine and Lucy had reached cuisine bliss.

"It's good to watch you eat. I like it," Vittorio said sitting back in his chair, swirling his wine in his glass. "As if you cannot get enough."

Lucy felt red heat spread across her face. She tried to calm herself as she wiped her mouth with a cloth napkin.

She had forgotten how incredible Italian food could taste. Most of the time she ate out of the vending machines at work. Chef Boyardee was one of her closest friends.

She had also forgotten how fantastic a torn piece of bread could be when its crust was sweet and warm from the oven, and the meat, sharp with spices, the melon, perfectly ripe and luscious, the olives, pungent with garlic.

Lucy had eaten everything and drunk all the wine until she felt so full she had to unbutton the top button of her pants.

She sat back. "I must have been hungry."

"You are starving," he said, and stared at her.

Lucy suddenly felt uncomfortable, as though he could hear her inner thoughts. She didn't like it. Didn't like it at all.

Antonio walked over. "The wine is ready, Vittorio."

"*Scusi*," Vittorio said to Lucy and got up from the table, picked up a box of wine and walked it out the back door. When he returned, it was time for farewell kisses and hugs.

"That was fantastic," Lucy told Vittorio when they were back in his car driving down the narrow motorway, her feet resting on the box of wine. "Thanks."

"You are welcome," he said with a little bow.

Lucy sat back in her seat and immediately fell asleep. It didn't take long before Vittorio made another stop.

This time he made his way through a tiny village to a farm where two ostriches stared at them from behind a tall wire fence and water buffalos poked their heads through wooden rails painted pure white, and a proud rooster spread its colorful head feathers in welcome.

"What now?" Lucy asked, all dreamy-eyed as Vittorio pulled the car up in front of a stone farmhouse. She was at once angry over another stop and fascinated by the farm surroundings.

"Garlic and mozzarella. The best! Wait 'til you taste the mozzarella. Fresh from early this morning. Sweet like mother's milk," he said and kissed his fingers again. This time Lucy smiled over at him as he made his way around the car to get her door. She waited, feeling a little woozy. She wanted to get mad because of the second delay, but all she could think of was the fresh mozzarella. The very thought of the creamy soft cheese made her mouth water in anticipation.

Inside the farmhouse, which turned out to be a busy restaurant, Lucy and Vittorio were greeted by a crusty middle-aged man with rough hands and a mustache that curled up at the ends. *"Vittorio! Ciao! Come va?"* the man asked as they hugged and kissed.

"Lucia, this is my cousin, Philippi." Philippi turned and hugged and kissed Lucy as if they were old friends. His mustache tickled and she saw a sly sparkle in his bright blue eyes. She thought this was getting too weird, like some episode of *The Sopranos*. All she needed now was for James Gandolfini to walk out of the back room pointing a gun at Vittorio and she'd know this was one of her sleepwalking episodes.

But he didn't.

Instead, she and Vittorio were escorted to a table next to a window with a view of the surrounding lush green hills. Black goats and white sheep grazed on the slopes, along with a few speckled cows.

Lucy wondered what it would be like to wake up every morning to see goats and cows out your back window instead of miles of beige stucco.

*"Scusi*, Lucia. I will return in a moment."

"More wine?"

"Fresh garlic. Mozzarella."

"You have a big family or something?"

"The biggest!"

Vittorio left her alone at the table. She refused to eat.

Absolutely refused, except for maybe a small piece of fresh mozzarella, and a mushroom or two.

And maybe a vegetable and a chunk of bread.

But that was it.

"Just a taste," she told the waitress.

Lucy tried to refuse the large plate of food the waitress brought over, until she saw what was on it—sliced tomatoes and fresh milky-white mozzarella drizzled with olive oil and herbs, grilled zucchini, mushrooms and eggplant. She couldn't resist. A loaf of bread appeared, and a carafe of red wine.

She thought she would simply taste the mozzarella and leave the rest, but once the sweet, rich cheese hit her tastebuds the battle was over. She took another bite and another until once again, she couldn't stop. She ate everything.

Meanwhile, she watched as Vittorio carried cartons of cheese out to the car.

When he joined her, Philippi appeared with two bowls of ravioli filled with goat's milk ricotta and artichoke hearts, smothered in a thick red sauce.

Lucy cringed.

"I can't eat anymore. I'm going to burst," she told Vittorio.

"You have to taste the ricotta. It is like nowhere else in the world," Vittorio said as he sliced open one of the round pillows of pasta revealing the soft cheese tucked inside. He poked one half of the pillow with his fork and held it up, cupping his other hand under the fork while the sauce dripped to his fingers.

"Come on," he urged, with a tilt of his head. Lucy leaned in and wrapped her lips around the ravioli, slowly pulling back to let the warm pasta with the luscious sauce fall into her mouth. Sauce dripped from her lips and onto Vittorio's fingers. He pulled his hand back and licked off the drops of sauce.

Lucy flushed and wiped her mouth with the back of her hand.

"What you think? *Buono?*" Vittorio sat back and watched as she ate, obviously enjoying the look of satisfaction on her face.

"Too good," she whispered under her breath.

# 5

"I THINK I'm going to be sick," Lucy said as Vittorio pulled her suitcase through the plush lobby of the Santa Maria hotel, a lavishly decked-out retreat with huge vases filled with fresh flowers, French gold-leafed tables and chairs. Red rugs with intricate colorful patterns running through thick fibers covered the brown-tiled floor, and marble pillars touched an ornate ceiling. A gigantic crystal chandelier hung right in the middle, shooting its rainbow of colors throughout the entire room.

The lobby was positively spectacular, and Lucy was positively mortified.

"What do you mean, sick?" he asked.

"I mean sick, like, I'm going to vomit. I have to get out of here," she whispered.

"No. Wait. We find a toilet," he said, but Lucy was on her way out the front door where she stopped to throw up...in front of the doorman...in front of a woman wearing a pink silk suit, and pink Christian Dior heels.

"*Dio mio!*" the woman yelled and took a step back. But it was too late. Lucy had let go with such a force that it splattered on the woman's dress and on her shoes.

"I'm sorry," Lucy murmured when it was all over, but the woman was so utterly disgusted she wouldn't even look up. The doorman ordered Lucy to leave as he ushered the screaming woman inside the lobby, away from Lucy who was now on a wobbly retreat. Fortunately the Alfa Romeo was parked right in front of the hotel. Completely humiliated, she got into the car, grateful that Vittorio had left it open.

"Ah yes, that kind of sick," Vittorio said. He returned her suitcase to the trunk and got in beside her. "You want I should get you some Briosci?"

"God! Can we just get out of here?" Lucy said as she slid down in her seat.

"But your room—"

Lucy looked at him, pleading. "I can't go in there now. Not after I just puked my guts out on some lady's shoes. And they were such pretty shoes."

Vittorio started the car and pulled away from the hotel.

Lucy's whole world spun around in a wild, mind-numbing tumble. She felt so thoroughly out of control she couldn't center on what she should do next, let alone where she should go. She desperately wanted to get away from Vittorio, but she couldn't quite focus on the how.

Fatigue engulfed her. If she could just close her eyes for a minute, maybe the world would stop spinning.

LUCY AWOKE like a kitten waking from a nap in the sun. She yawned and stretched as sunlight played in colored shapes on the windows and dashboard. She had a slight headache, but mostly felt completely at ease and at peace with herself as she looked around for what caused the sunlight to dance, but she couldn't find it. Perhaps the rental had come with a crystal, she thought. How fabulous.

She hadn't slept as well or as soundly in a very long time and she relished the moment. Only, something was wrong. She was sitting in the passenger side of the car and not the driver's side. How odd. And, she could smell coffee. How could that be? And onions. She could actually smell onions frying.

"What time is it?" she said, and moved out of her almost fetal position to look at her watch.

As she moved, her eyes shut with a deep yawn, her arms encircled the man sleeping next to her, warm and responsive. Maybe she wasn't awake, after all, she mused. She felt him pull her in closer. She liked the way he made her feel when her body touched his. Liked the smell of him, the warmth. She especially liked the way his arms felt around her. "Lucia," he said in a low voice as his lips lingered next to hers for a moment before sending a sensual shiver through her entire body. His breath warm on her throat...

"It's you," she yelled, eyes now wide open.

With all the strength in her legs and arms, she pushed Vittorio right out of the open car door and onto the street. He landed next to a fruit stand and tomatoes cascaded onto his head. Lucy jumped out of the car.

Total panic swept over her, causing her head to throb and her stomach to ache as she stood next to the car and realized she had no idea where she was.

"You are the lowest of the low. Pond scum, that's what you are. Pond scum," Lucy said as she struggled to get her things out of the car. The street was crowded with people, so Lucy tried to keep her voice down.

"Lucia, what is wrong? I did nothing," Vittorio said as he gingerly stood, avoiding the tomatoes.

They stared at each other from either side of the sports car. The hood glistened in the sunshine, giving everything a sort of red glow. Lucy said, "You were about to kiss me."

"Yes."

"What else happened while I was sleeping? Wait...I don't want to know. Yes. I do. No. I don't." Total panic sent her spinning out of control.

"Lucia, nothing happened. You have my word."

"Your word! Is that supposed to mean something? Do we have some sort of history I can pin that statement on to?"

"Lucia, of course you know me. We just slept together," he said, grinning.

"We did *not* sleep together. That was a rest, a nap, nothing more."

"But Lucia, you are so beautiful when you are in my arms."

"You are the most despicable, contemptible...there are no words to describe you. You're beyond words. You're a thing. A slimy, green thing."

"Please. Be calm. What could I do? Your jacket was wet, and stained."

Her jacket? What jacket? Lucy suddenly realized she wasn't wearing her white jacket. Things were digressing rapidly. Somehow in her fog, she remembered vomiting on some woman's shoes. Embarrassment washed over her like a mud bath, thick and warm, but she was determined not to let the pond scum know. Not now. Not in the middle of an argument.

"Okay, so what! You took advantage of me and I can't even remember all that we did, or if we did. Did we?"

He made a gesture indicating that she was being ridiculous. "Lucia, please," then he reached into the car, pulled out her jacket and scarf and handed them to her across the roof.

She ripped them out of his hands. The jacket stunk, and was covered in red wine stains. "You're so *typical.*"

"Lucia, do not be like this. Everything is fine."

Lucy seriously doubted that. What she needed was a restroom so she could clean herself up and leave. "I need a ladies' room," she said.

"*Scusi?*" He didn't understand her.

"A toilet. I need a public toilet," she explained.

"But my mamma's villa is not far. I have a nice room. We go there. You will be more comfortable."

Lucy had read somewhere that many Italian young men liked to live at home with their mothers, who doted on them as if they were still little boys, rather than moving out on their own. The Italians called them *mammisimos,* mamma's boys. She wondered if Vittorio was a *mammisimo.*

Probably, she thought. He has that mamma's-boy look.

Lucy spotted a public toilet sign down the street. "Can I please have my luggage out of the trunk? I need to get to Subito, like, now." She glanced at her watch. It was already one o'clock. "Damn, I'm late." He unloaded her luggage.

"*Scusi,* you gotta get to Subito?" Vittorio asked, slowly, as if he didn't believe what she had just said.

He was really an aggravating man. Did he know something about Subito?

Well, even if he did, she didn't care.

"Yes, and I'm going to be late for my own meeting."

"Subito. Your business is Subito?" Vittorio laughed.

"What's so funny?" she said, one hand clutching her suitcase, the other on her hip. He probably had a job there once, she thought, as the supplies manager, but spent most of his time driving around looking for just the right pencil, so they fired his ass and he's been resentful ever since. That's why he got me drunk, forced me to miss my meeting and kissed me. It's pure and simple sabotage!

"Lucia, I—"

But Lucy had no more time for him and his clever diversions. She went off down the street in a huff.

"I wait here, Lucia," he called after her, but Lucy had no intention of ever coming back. While she walked, she thought about Seth and how much she needed to talk to him. To see him. To prove that she really and truly loved him.

She pulled out her phone.

The call went right through as if he was just down the street. "Hello," he said.

"I don't want to wait for Saturday. Let's get married here. Tomorrow. You could hop on a plane today and we could be married in twenty-four hours. You never wanted an actual wedding anyway. It'll be fun. No relatives. No corny toasts. No reception lines. Just you and me. What do you say?"

"Lucy? Is that you? I can barely hear you."

"Yes. It's me. I want to get married tomorrow."

"Me too, babe."

"No, you don't understand. I *really* want to get married tomorrow. Here. You can fly here."

"Be serious. It's only a few more days. For one thing, I have an important project meeting that I'm leading on Friday morning." He yawned. "For another, you've got a chip to get out."

"I know, but couldn't we just this once do something crazy? Something romantic? I'll find some cute little church, they must have thousands of them here. Italians invented cute little churches. We'll get married as soon as you get here. Then we can have a real honeymoon. Two weeks in Positano. Doesn't that sound thrilling?"

"Sounds expensive. Look, babe, we'll have our whole lives to be crazy and romantic, right now we have our careers to think about. Besides, the wedding's a done deal. Can't change it now."

"But—"

"Hang in there, babe." He yawned again. A great big, loud yawn right into her ear. "Have an early-morning meeting. Got to get back to sleep. Later."

"I love you," she said, but he had already hung up.

The conversation didn't exactly go the way she had imagined, but he was probably right. He was always right, and logical. That's why she loved him so much, for his logic.

But somehow it sounded odd to be in love with a guy's logic. It was like being in love with an equation, a thought process, rather than an entire person. But it was better this way. Anything else would cancel out her empowerment.

And if there was one thing a twenty-seven-year-old female engineer needed, at least according to *Society of Women Engineers* magazine, it was to be empowered. It didn't matter if your personal life turned into a complete mess, as long as your career was on the High Performance Track, you were destined for success.

Her stomach growled. She couldn't possibly be hungry again. Could she?

She wanted no part of Italian food. If she was going to eat, she'd rather have a Balance bar and a Diet Coke. The perfect meal—fast, easy and efficient. You could eat it in the car on the way to work. No fuss. All your essential vitamins conveniently combined in a five-minute intake. Perfect.

She dragged her suitcase into a toilet with a door

that wouldn't lock. The place smelled funky and had a strange combination of an open stall, a urinal, a sink, a cracked and foggy mirror, and a public phone all crammed into a damp little room.

As it turned out, once Lucy had cleaned up and changed into a simple pair of black dress pants, which were already a little tight now that she had consumed enough food for an entire family of eight, and a white long-sleeved, cotton blouse, she felt like her old business-as-usual self again. She tucked the red scarf, which she had thought would be rather festive, and her white suit neatly into her suitcase, regretting ever having worn them, or for that matter, ever having bought them. She would give the red scarf to her mother as soon as she got back home.

So much for festive.

And she would burn the suit.

No more of this dependent woman crap. Whatever happened this morning would just have to slide into her past. Seth didn't really need to know. Not really, after all, nothing had happened. A kiss, maybe? Nothing more. She would never think of it nor mention it again. She would simply go on with her original plan. She'd grab a cab and drive away from this nightmare forever. Her life would go on as if this whole episode had never, ever happened.

She wanted nothing more to do with Vittorio. He was just a blip on life's screen. An insignificant speed bump on her road to success.

And a total pain in the ass.

# 6

LUCY SNEAKED DOWN the crowded alley without Vittorio noticing her. He was too busy arguing with the fruit-stand owner over the price of the tomatoes that had fallen on his head. Two other people, a man and a woman, stood arguing on the front steps of the townhouse across the small alley. Three other people watched. Right next to them, a flower merchant argued with a customer over the price of daisies and down the block to her right, two men argued over the freshness of a display of garlic. There were people everywhere in this tight neighborhood, bickering, gyrating, and yelling out their passions. The theatrical spectacle of emotion was in full production.

She guessed she might be in the *Spaccanapoli* district, the heart of *Napoli*. It didn't matter. She didn't care that she had heard about this place countless times, there would be no looking around. No searching for street signs, nor landmarks, nor anything that might guide her back to the neighborhood, Vittorio's neighborhood, just in case she was tempted to try to find it again, later.

Not that she ever would, but just in case.

Nope, she just wanted out. Away from. Never to go back to. And never to think of Vittorio again. Ever.

After a relatively short walk, Lucy found a cab sitting in front of a small hotel. As soon as she got in she knew this was not going to be an easy drive. Her clues were the orange-and-black Tony Stewart cap the driver wore and the Jeff Gordon jacket on the seat next to him.

As she gave Mr. NASCAR the address on *Via de Mille* in the *Chiaia* district, she strapped herself in. He peeled rubber just pulling away from the curb. This was a drag race with every other Neapolitan who dared to venture out on the crowded, blustering streets. She tried not to look as the driver cut people off, drove up curbs and then down a railroad track with a train visibly heading right for them, all of which seemed not to rattle him in the least. His complete focus was on his driving, as though this was an actual race and he wanted to win the Winston Cup.

Lucy screamed, "Look out," when a woman stepped out in front of their car. He swerved up on the sidewalk to get around her, nearly clipping a guy parking a motor scooter. Mr. NASCAR stuck his head out the window to yell at the woman who had so stupidly walked in front of him. She snapped her thumbnail on her front teeth to tell him to go to hell and continued to cross the street, causing another car to swerve out of her way.

Lucy's pulse raced, her hands hurt from holding onto the door handle, as if that could stop her from dying when he hit some immovable object, and her seatbelt was so tight she could hardly breathe. Her whole body was a mass of tension and stress.

The driver slammed on the brakes. For a moment Lucy didn't react. Couldn't react. He said. "We are here."

"Hmm?" she moaned.

"This is Subito."

"Subito?" she asked turning to look at him.

"Yes. We are here." He got out of the car to go around and get her suitcase out of the trunk. Lucy slowly let go of the handle and massaged the blood back into her hands. Her door opened.

"Thank you," she muttered. She really wanted to yell at him, say some nasty Italian curse that would make his soul tremble, but she didn't have the strength to think. Instead, she stepped out of the cab, paid him with American money, grabbed hold of her things and slowly walked toward the satellite company she had actually been ordered, er, volunteered to save. She seriously wondered about her sanity.

The cab sped away behind her, horns blaring as he pulled back into the endless race.

Lucy straightened out her collar, tucked in her blouse and walked to the front door of the historic building on one of the busiest streets in Naples. Blue blinds covered the windows, and a religious shrine adorned one of the walls. The word *Subito* flashed in a matching blue on the neon sign above the door. It looked more like a bordello than an electronics company.

She grabbed the front-door knob to yank it open. It didn't budge. Like it should just be open, she thought. She dug out her badge from her purse, punched in her code on the black electronic security pad next to the door and swiped.

Nothing.

Okay, so maybe she punched in the wrong numbers. Could happen. She slowly punched in her code again, and swiped her badge. Slowly.

Nothing. No beep. No click-click when the door unlocked. Nothing but street noise. Obviously, her code didn't work at this site, so she knocked. No response. She knocked harder until her knuckles hurt. Again nothing. Perhaps they were holding the meeting without her and didn't want to be disturbed. Or they were eating lunch, a pizza no doubt, smothered in anchovies and fresh buffalo mozzarella. And why not? Neapolitans served up the best pizza in the world. Didn't they invent pizza?

She reigned in her pizza thoughts and concentrated on the task of getting inside the building.

Lucy thought it strange that there wasn't a receptionist available or even that secretary who had made her flight reservations and arranged for her pass entry. What was her name? She couldn't remember, but it began with *R*. She was never much good with names—a bad habit more than anything else—one of those things that had never seemed very important to her.

Although lately, with all the traveling around to various sites and meetings with customers, she thought she'd better change her laziness. This time she would memorize their names. Make up little poems. Say them over and over again...where the hell was everybody?

She paced, back and forth, back and forth. An hour went by and still nothing. She sat on the stoop and dialed Subito's main number. No one answered so she left a message. "This is Lucy Mastronardo. I'm standing outside your front door and can't get in. Could someone please let me in? Thanks."

She stood up and waited directly in front of the door, thinking that someone would come out at any moment. No one came.

She phoned again. This time she called Giovanni. "I'm sorry to bother you, but I can't seem to get in.

Could you please send someone out to the front door? Thanks. Oh, this is Lucy Mastronardo."

She faced the door, expecting it to open with an apologetic Giovanni sucking up to her, begging forgiveness, making the excuse that they were so involved with work, they weren't answering any phones today. Or the receptionist had been hit by a bus just that morning and they were frantically trying to find a replacement, but there was a shortage of good receptionists in *Napoli* this time of year because all the pretty young women had moved to Vegas to become strippers.

She wanted to scream. But once again, the door didn't move.

It was now three o'clock. Lucy had rolled up her sleeves, clipped up her hair, had left countless messages and still no one had opened the front door. Granted, it had been lunchtime when she arrived. That would account for an hour, but what about the rest of the time?

Perhaps it was a holiday? But they had a chip to get out in less than a week, so why would they take a holiday now?

The day had heated up and gotten humid in the process, very humid. She felt as if her clothes were glued on. Her head was pounding. She took an aspirin. Several aspirins.

Her stomach felt empty and ached because of all the aspirin. She wanted to pass out from the heat, the exhaust fumes. She wondered if anyone would care? Would anyone notice? The street had quieted. Christ, were they all home sleeping? Did they still do that *pausa* thing? Certainly not at Subito, they knew better than to keep those medieval traditions.

Mad now, Lucy phoned the main number again. Her phone was on the verge of death, ready to fade into powerlessness, but she got in one last message. "Look. This is ridiculous! Where the hell are you people? I'm standing out here sucking up exhaust fumes and you guys are...who knows what the hell you're doing. Come out here right now and let me in!" Her phone went dead.

She waited. She yelled.

She sat down on the stoop, opened her laptop and sent threatening memos to the people inside. She sent e-mails to her bosses. Their bosses. Her mother. Seth.

It was three-thirty.

She took a tranquilizer.

Somewhere around four o'clock, a young woman showed up. She carried several small shopping bags and a large hatbox. By this time, Lucy wanted to give up the battle and find a room, but the girl—who wore an outfit appropriate for a summer picnic—a really short green skirt, floral halter top, no stockings and stiletto sandals—threw her arms around Lucy and gave her a kiss on each cheek. "Hi," she said. "You must be Lucy. We're so excited that you're here."

"And you are?" Lucy asked, pulling herself away.

The girl stuck a key into the door and stepped inside. "Come on in. I hope you haven't been standing there long. I try to get back first to meet the FedEx guy, but there was the best sale at this little *orario continuato* shop down the street. It's one of those rare shops that doesn't close for lunch." She stopped to check out Lucy's outfit. "Oh, you've got to go. You'll die in those clothes. This is Naples. You can't wear that silly business stuff here. It's too hot and chic for business drab."

Drab! When had she turned *drab?* Lucy stepped inside.

"I'm Rosalyn Milton from the heart of rock 'n' roll."

"Cleveland?"

"You're good. Yeah, I used to work at the Hall of Fame. Met a lot of cool musicians, old, but still cool. I'm a sucker for a guy with a guitar."

"What do you do here?"

"Sort of the office manager-receptionist-human resource and travel lady. We spoke on the phone. I booked your flight and stuff. If you need anything, I can usually find it. I guess everything was okay with your itinerary, 'cause you're here," she said, all smiley.

Lucy wanted to yell at her about the window-seat mix-up, the car disaster and all her many other woes, but now was not the time. "Where is everybody?" Lucy asked as Rosalyn threw her keys and tiny purse down on a desk in what seemed to be the lobby.

"At lunch."

"What?"

"They should be back soon. But it's hot out there today, so it might be a little later, depending on when they wake up."

"Wake up?"

"Aren't you Italian?"

"What's that got to do with anything?"

"This is Italy. Remember? Lunches take two to three hours, depending on the food intake. And lately, the intake has been...I used to wear a size zero, now it's a four. How long are you going to be here?"

"Five days, but—"

"You'll gain at least three pounds. Maybe more, if you eat dinner at nine o'clock the way everyone else does. It's amazing that there are any skinny people at all in this country." She pressed the button on the answering machine and listened as Lucy's voice echoed orders and demands.

Lucy cringed. "You can just skip right through all of those."

"You must have been out there a long time," Rosalyn said, as she hit the skip button over and over again, until she came to a male voice, all mellow and sexy, "Hey, baby, last night was magic. How 'bout tonight? Mmm, I want more. Call me."

"Your boyfriend?" Lucy asked.

"No. Just some after-dinner mint I met last night. You should have gone to the restaurant next door while you were waiting. That's where everyone goes at lunchtime. Fabulous food! There's a little garden out back where—"

"I'm not hungry," Lucy snapped. She was angry now, angry at this airhead girl and the rest of this company of slackers. "Where do I sign in?" she asked, resting her things down on the floor in front of the desk.

"Nowhere. It's a small company. I know everybody," Rosalyn said without missing a beat. "Let me show you your office. You can use Frank Leon's." Lucy picked up her suitcase and her laptop as Rosalyn continued. "It's just around the corner. Frank went to Colombia to visit his family for a few weeks and was captured or something by the rebels. Anyway, his father's paid the ransom so we're waiting to hear. Giovanni thought you might want to use his office since it has the best view."

"Frank's been kidnapped? Isn't that dangerous?"

"I don't know. They say it happens every year. Nobody gets too upset."

"Isn't Frank your only I.T. guy? What if there's a system problem before tape-out? Who's your back-up?"

"You know this industry. If you wait for a chip to go out, you'll never get a vacation."

Somehow, Lucy didn't think getting kidnapped in Colombia warranted the word *vacation*, but that wasn't what bugged her. It was the fact that somebody as important as Frank had been allowed to leave in the first place.

They walked through an open doorway and down a narrow hallway with more open doorways to the right. When Lucy peeked in she could see about eight or nine Sun Workstations set up along the walls on long brown tables. There seemed to be three rooms like this, and three more private offices to her left and a sign directly in front of her that read Toilet. The uneven plaster walls were painted a light yellow, but each room was a different shade of faded green, orange or blue.

When they arrived at Frank's office, it was a mess of papers, books and clutter. The desk, with another workstation, faced a bank of three open windows, and the noise from the busy street below echoed so loudly that it seemed as though she was still out on the sidewalk. Lucy didn't actually believe anyone could work in here. Besides all the noise, it was hot. Very hot.

"Is this a great office or what?" Rosalyn asked, smiling.

Great office! It must be that bright red streak in her black hair. She was obviously delusional. Lucy smiled, and walked over to the desk to put her things down.

"I need a room. Would it be too much trouble for you to get me one?" Lucy asked.

"Not a problem. We usually book at the Santa Maria."

Lucy wanted no part of the Santa Maria. "I can't... I don't... Is there another hotel around here?"

"You betcha, but there's the *Santa Restituita* festival this week. It's pretty great. They have an amazing boat procession in the bay. You ought to check it out while you're here. Anyway, all the hotels are probably booked, but I know this incredible guy at the Santa Maria. I'll give him a call."

"Another after-dinner mint?"

"No. More of an appetizer."

That actually made Lucy smile, but she still didn't want any part of that hotel. "I have my reasons for not wanting the Santa Maria. Anything else would be great."

"You could share my flat. My roomy's gone for another week. It's just down the block."

Lucy was hesitant. She really wanted her own room. "Thanks, but—"

"I'll see what I can do." Rosalyn started to leave then stepped back in the office. "I'm going out to get an espresso. Want one?"

"Isn't there a coffeemaker?"

Rosalyn shook her head. "We had one around here somewhere, but it broke about a year ago and we never got it fixed. Besides, no one ever used it. There's a great espresso bar right next door. We have a tab."

"A tab?"

"Yeah. Isn't it great?"

Lucy tried to shut one of the windows. Rosalyn stopped her. "There's no air-conditioning so you might want to reconsider that. It can get extreme in here. So, did you want a coffee?"

"Latte, thanks...with cocoa."

"Anything else? They have some awesome biscotti and pastries."

"Just the latte."

"You betcha! Oh, and if the FedEx guy shows up, just sign for it and leave whatever it is on my desk. I'll take care of it when I get back. Thanks."

When she left, Lucy stared out the window, listening to the cars and city noise, trying to get used to it all.

It was four o'clock Monday afternoon, and of Subito's twenty-some employees only the receptionist had decided to show up after lunch...and she was off getting coffee "on the tab!"

What was that all about?

# 7

THE EMPLOYEES trickled in sometime after four-thirty. A few of them stopped by Lucy's new office to greet her.

"Hello," a middle-aged black woman said, extending her hand to Lucy. Lucy grabbed hold and shook. "I'm Debra, one of the engineers. We're very happy you're here. No one from the States ever comes out. You're the first one. It's so nice." Debra had a Jamaican accent and spoke slow and soft. Lucy had to move in closer just to hear her. "Will you be staying long?" she whispered.

"Actually, no, I have to be back home by Friday night. I'm hoping the chip will go out by Thursday," Lucy said.

Debra let go of her hand and took a step back. Then she started talking, but with all the noise out the window, Lucy couldn't hear a word. Debra did, however, look a lot like Diana Ross, so it was delightful to watch her speak, hands gesturing, head bobbing, almost as if she were on stage against the backdrop of the windows and the blue sky. Lucy leaned in to listen. "That's when I..." but her voice drifted off again. Lucy smiled and nodded a few times, but she had absolutely no idea what Debra was saying.

There was a break in the street noise and Debra said, "I'm glad you agree. I'll be looking forward to it."

To what? Lucy had no clue what she had just agreed to.

Debra held out her hand again. Lucy took it and said, "I'd like to discuss this again sometime."

"Sure. Anytime. Nice meeting you," Debra said, and walked out of the office.

Fine, Lucy thought, what the hell did she just say?

Before she had time to think about it, two more employees wandered in, a young guy, obviously Italian, about Lucy's age, baggy-chic clothes, shaggy hair. The other guy Chinese, with intense smokey-blue eyes hidden behind Armani glasses, and a wide, friendly smile. His hair was short and messy with thin sideburns, a Brad Pitt with an Asian flair. "Hi," the Italian said. "I'm Joe Strano and this is Joe Yoo. Engineers."

"Hi," Lucy said, happy they had the same simple name. How could she forget the two Joes?

"We're just in the other room," Joe S. said.

"Yeah, if you need anything, just come by," Joe Y. said, leaning on the doorjamb, his arms folded against his obviously rippled chest. He wore a thin white shirt and black jeans. These two guys were nothing like the engineers at B-Logic, not a Dilbert trait in sight.

"Thanks," she said. "I will." The thought crossed her mind of how hot Joe Y. must be in bed. He had a great body, even if he was only five-three.

As they were leaving, another man walked in, tall, about six-foot-five, wearing blue socks, sandals, tan shorts, and a blue T-shirt with an open, patterned dress shirt over the whole combo.

"Who are you?" he said with an accent Lucy couldn't place. "Are you replacing Frank?" He spoke in Italian, but she could tell it wasn't his native language. She thought she'd try English.

"No," she said. "I'm from B-Logic. I'm here to—"

"You're our watchdog," he said in English.

"Well, actually—"

"Actually, you're here to make sure we're doing our job. Sort of makes you the villain, don't it?"

"I never thought of—"

"Didn't need to send you. We know what we have to do. But now that you're here, what can you do?"

"Well, I—"

"You push paper around, don't you? Can you do layout, 'cause that's what we need right now. Somebody to help with layout, DRC, LVS."

"I used to—"

"Technology changes too fast for 'used to.' I guess that means you don't know the process."

"I'm not as—"

"Have a nice visit," he said and disappeared.

Lucy sat down hard in her chair, a green cloth thing with a thin, uncomfortable seat. Not exactly the ergonomic masterpiece she had back home. She suddenly longed for the ergonomic efficiency of her chair, and the solace of blue cubicles. There was something comforting about blue, something steadfast, solid and true...blue.

That's when the classic Italian beauty waddled into the office looking at once lovely and very pregnant in her blue dress. Lucy immediately stood up, thinking she should offer her a chair or a glass of water.

"Ciao," she said, holding the right side of her back. "I'm Isabella, the layout designer." She held out her other hand. Lucy took it and guided her to the uncomfortable green chair. "Thanks. It's getting harder and harder to stand," she said rubbing her large, round belly. Isabella was a tiny creature with a huge belly beneath her Laura Ashley dress. She looked as if she had swallowed a basketball. Everything else on her tiny body was trim and slim, except for her tummy.

"Ciao," Lucy said. "Nice to meet you."

Isabella was indeed beautiful, with rich brown hair that tumbled to her waist, deep-olive skin, and dark-brown eyes, but she had something else that wasn't Italian, or at least not local Italian. No real accent.

"I'm so glad you're here. I keep sending e-mails to the main office, but no one listens to me. I've heard some nice things about you. Maybe you'll understand my concerns. The chip is close to being clean, but there are some rule issues that no one wants to address. It's the via coverage rule on the top level of the chip. It's causing me all sorts of problems. A real nightmare that I can't seem to solve on my own. Are we going to have a meeting?"

"Yes, as soon as possible. I'd like to get the status."

"Terrific. We'll discuss it then."

Isabella stood to leave. Lucy helped her up. It took a lot for her to get out of the chair.

"Where are you from? You don't seem to have an accent," Lucy asked.

"You probably don't remember me, but I used to work at B-Logic."

Lucy tried to remember, but couldn't. "I'm sorry," she said.

"I was part of orientation on your first day. I looked a lot different then: short hair, business-wear, glasses. I was into that whole Silicon Valley thing. A slave to deadlines. Then this job came up and I applied and got it. Met my husband, Mario, got pregnant and never looked back."

Somewhere way in a dark corner of Lucy's memory,

she remembered meeting a tough-looking woman on that first day, but it couldn't have been Isabella. That woman was as rigid as a nail and had absolutely no sense of humor. She had told Lucy all about the company and how many hours they expected from their exempt employees, about ethics and dress codes and, actually, after the talk, Lucy had gone into the ladies room to vomit.

This couldn't be the same woman.

Isabella continued. "I was born in *Napoli* and lived here until I was nine. My parents are in the military so we moved around a lot, but my heart has always been here in Italy. Anyway, I'm really looking forward to working with you. Never got the chance the first time around. I left about a week after I gave you that speech on hours and dress codes."

And that's when Lucy recognized her, when Isabella said *dress codes* her voice changed. It got harsh, the way it had been on that first day.

How could someone so uptight and nasty change into someone so sweet and Laura Ashley?

"Yep, it's me." Looking down, she rubbed her belly. "We'll be in my office. Just holler if you need anything."

She walked away, leaving behind a really bad memory.

AT FIVE O'CLOCK Lucy was finally able to hold her meeting.

Giovanni, a tall middle-aged man with a fascination for fishing, apparent from the pictures on his office walls and the Hawaiian fish shirt he wore, officially introduced her to the team.

He spoke in English to a crowded, hot room with not enough green chairs.

"We are honored today by the presence of Lucia Mastronardo, program manager, from our home office in Sunnyvale, America," he said.

Everyone applauded.

Lucy stood next to Giovanni, blushing. She felt as if she were on stage instead of heading a project meeting, which she had done a thousand times before. Suddenly, she wanted to recite a poignant speech or at least say something funny.

But all she could say was, "Thanks."

They applauded again.

She could tell this was not going to be easy. They were far too eager to please.

How could she possibly get them to do what she wanted if they were so thrilled with her presence? Wasn't that management rule number one or something? Never become friends with your subordinates. At least that's what her boss would tell her, but she wasn't her boss and these weren't exactly her subordinates. Just a group of people who, by their actions, could either gain her a promotion or cause her to remain at her present status—a wannabe.

When they finally stopped, she began her pep talk. "I think I met most of you earlier, but it's nice to see you again."

That was dumb, she thought. She cleared her throat and took a sip of S. Pellegrino water, which Rosalyn had provided. She continued. "Anyway, I know how hard you've all been working."

More applause.

She waited.

"I appreciate your enthusiasm, really I do, but could

you please hold the applause. Thanks," she said and looked around at their now-joyless faces and felt as if she had just taken away their balloons.

She went on. "I'm here to help you guys get the S9293 out by the end of the week. Whatever problems you have with tools, programs or process I'm here to act as your conduit to solve the problem. Also, I think we're going to have to reconsider the long lunches."

The guy with the blue socks coughed and mumbled something. She couldn't catch it, but whatever it was, the two Joes snickered.

She kept talking despite the interruption. "I've made up a schedule for the week," she said as she passed it out to the employees. "I've gone ahead and broken up the tasks according to what's left on the top level. If we stick to this schedule we should be able to tape-out on Friday. But the engineers have to stop making changes. Today is the last day for any changes. If you don't give them to layout by midnight tonight, we'll have to put them on the re-spin."

Debra politely interrupted.

The room got quiet as everyone leaned toward her. It seemed as though the entire building had just tipped. "According to this schedule, you have us working from eight in the morning until ten or eleven at night."

"Yes, I kind of left that open to your discretion."

Blue Socks asked, "So, you have us set up to work fourteen-hour days, with a half hour for lunch. Is that right?"

"Yes. I'd like to hold a status meeting first thing every morning. I realize that it seems like it still won't be enough time to get everything done, but we all have to sleep sometime," Lucy said, expecting everyone to agree, or to laugh or at the very least throw a shoe, but the room fell silent. Even the street noise disappeared. "Anyway, I'm here to make sure we hit our deadline. Are there any questions?"

No one moved. She looked at Isabella, expecting a question, an issue, but Isabella looked down at the schedule and ignored her.

"Okay then," Lucy said. "We'll go over each item that still needs to be done to get an idea of how many hours it will take. Please refer to page two of your schedule. I've highlighted the tasks that need to be completed by the end of the day. We'll need a complete bypass and timing review. I'll need the Verilog simulation status and the power distribution or current density complete for each block. The via density needs to be addressed, and the PLL noise/shielding review really needs to take place this evening if we expect to go out on Friday.

"Also, tomorrow, please present top-level interface timing with extracted BA. This should include bus drop from the power-supply pads to each block and signal swing changes due to internal block drops." She looked up. "Please take the time to review the items completed on the next few pages. If any of these items are not actually complete, please e-mail me the time and date of their intended completion. Are there any questions?"

Everyone flipped through the thick document, glancing at it, but not really looking at it.

It was the first time in Lucy's career she felt majorly judged standing in front of her contemporaries, as if they were millworkers or stockbrokers and she was speaking the wrong lingo.

No one said a word, so Lucy continued with the meeting, even though her stomach was churning and she was developing one of those monumental headaches that only another tranquilizer could cure.

She carried on anyway and hoped she wouldn't collapse on the tiny table. With the current attitude in the room, there was no telling how they might react.

Sometime around seven-thirty the meeting broke for dinner. There was plenty more Lucy wanted to cover, but the team complained of being hungry.

"We can continue this tomorrow morning. You guys have plenty to do tonight after dinner," she said, and no sooner had the words left her lips than everyone stormed out, leaving their schedules on the table in the middle of the room. Even Isabella passed her by without so much as a "catch ya later."

Lucy decided to call her boss, Dennis, with an update and get something quick—Cheetos and a Diet Coke—the perfect working-girl dinner—out of the vending machine. Only she couldn't quite remember where it was.

She left the small conference room to look for it, retracing her steps, but unless there was another floor, she couldn't find it.

Like, they didn't have a vending machine! Every company had a vending machine. It was the law or something. How else could an overworked employee function?

Lucy poked her head in the lobby. "Rosalyn, where's our vending machines?"

"Don't have any."

"What?"

"We don't have any vending machines."

"Don't people complain? Don't they get hungry?"

"They go out."

"To get a candy bar?"

"They don't eat candy."

"Everybody eats candy."

"Not the kind that comes from a machine." She picked up her purse and stood up. "It's time for me to get out of here. I'm going next door. You want to come?"

"What's next door?" Lucy remembered. "Oh, that's right, the garden room with the company tab."

"Yeah, you'll love the owner. He's one deliciously hot guy. He's been away for a few weeks at a culinary conference. I think he's looking to open another restaurant. We're having a welcome home party for him tonight. You should come."

"Another appetizer?"

"Mmm, no. He's more the main course," she purred.

Lucy thought about all the food she had eaten that morning and decided she couldn't even think of Italian food, let alone eat any, besides, her pants were still tight and uncomfortable. "No thanks. I've got a lot to do around here. Oh, did you find me a room?"

"Nope. I guess you're stuck with me."

Lucy wasn't very happy. Of all the people in all the world. "That's great, actually. Really, great." Lucy smiled at her new roomy.

Argh!

"Come over and get me when you're ready. See ya," Rosalyn said and left.

Lucy walked back to her office. The place was completely deserted. She would have to say something about this when everyone returned. How could they ever expect to get the job done if they didn't work through dinner?

# 8

"Hey, babe, how's it goin'?" Seth asked. He sounded rushed.

"It's goin'," Lucy answered as she shifted the phone from one ear to the other. She was busy checking the latest layout-verses schematic run. Isabella had made it seem as though she was close to having the chip clean, that the layout matched the schematic, but when Lucy checked the Calibre report, there were still some five hundred errors on the top level of the chip.

"Are you cracking the whip?"

"I'm trying, but so far I don't seem to be getting anywhere. I think they're not used to working so hard."

"You know how those Italians are."

"No. How are they?" she snapped.

"Lighten up. That was a joke. I was agreeing with what you were saying."

She let it go. "I know. Miss me?"

"Hmm?"

"I said, do you miss me?" She was looking for a "yeah. I'm dying without you. Can't go on another minute. When will you be home?" But instead she got....

"Sure, babe. Oh, I ordered a fountain of mai tai mix for the reception."

"You? Was it expensive?"

"Not really. It's this great big glass fountain that sits

in the middle of the table and spews out mai tais. You take your glass and fill it up under one of the streams. Really cool. Of course, I may have some trouble convincing your mother. She wants a tower of struffella, whatever that is."

"Honey anisette cookies. They're a tradition with our family."

"They sound awful. I think the mai tai fountain is a great idea, don't you?"

Lucy was confused. Seth, who never even wanted an actual wedding, who wanted to go to Vegas and get married to save time, was suddenly ordering mai tai fountains. "What's going on, Seth?"

"What do you mean?"

"A mai tai fountain? *You* want a mai tai fountain?"

"Look, babe, I gotta go. I've got a presentation this afternoon and I still haven't made my foils. Since they laid off all the secretaries, it's been hell. I'll call you later. See ya."

And that was it.

"See ya?" she said out loud. "Fine!" She put the phone down in its receiver and stared at it for a moment, wondering what was going on with him.

The clock on Frank's desk said ten o'clock and Subito was still deserted, except for her. She was suddenly too tired to think about fountains, Seth or work. She let out a big yawn, and her stomach growled at the same time. She couldn't concentrate anymore.

Actually, she hadn't been able to fully concentrate all day. All she could think about was Vittorio. She wondered where he was right then. How warm and loving it had felt when he had pulled her in closer. And how delicious he had smelled. Some part of her had known it wasn't Seth, but she hadn't wanted to admit it. Still didn't want to admit it.

She wished she could remember why she had allowed herself to think it was all right to be wrapped in some other guy's arms, but she never remembered the details of her semi-dreams, even when she was a kid and would sleepwalk. She had lied when she'd told her mother it didn't happen anymore. It happened all the time, especially when she was stressed, which was every day. Sometimes it would get so bad she would wake up in her kitchen under the table, or curled up in the shower. But it would all end as soon as she married Seth. Being married would eliminate all her stress.

Or not.

She was way too hungry to think about that now, and much too tired. All she wanted was something quick to eat and a bed to fall into—a big comfortable bed in a private room at the Santa Maria.

The thought of sharing a room with Rosalyn made her cringe. She could only hope it would be for one night. She could take almost any inconvenience for one night. She gathered her stuff and turned out the light.

Accordion music filled the air as Lucy walked up to the front door of La Bella Note, a seemingly tiny restaurant right next door.

The sign was about the size of a slice of bread, and the front door looked like an open gate to someone's front yard.

Who knew?

Once she stepped inside, the music intensified, as did the laughter and general chatter bouncing off the brick walls. It was as if she were walking into an opera house with unbelievable acoustics. The restaurant was an ultramodern Italian eating palace, where glass, chrome and leather mixed well with black, white and tan to give off the mood of comfortable luxury.

She spotted Rosalyn sitting at a long table in the back with some of the other employees, Giovanni being one of them. His shirt looked luminescent in the mixture of red and green lights of the crowded restaurant. He stood, ready to greet her at the table.

"Lucy, over here," Rosalyn yelled.

Lucy waved back and made her way through the crowd.

"This place is amazing," Lucy said and took a deep breath. The smell of spicy Italian food permeated the air and reminded her of her mother's kitchen.

A sense of absolute hunger swept over her. She couldn't wait to eat. She sat down in the empty chair next to Rosalyn and reached over to pull off a chunk of bread from the loaf in the middle of the table.

"Ah, Lucia, you finally made it," a voice said from behind her, a voice that sounded very familiar. She turned around slowly, thinking about what she would say. *It's you, you womanizer. You home-wrecker. You cad. Are you stalking me? Waiting until I got out of work to make your move? What? You have something to say? Let me give you a piece of my mind, you miserable son of a...*

But it was Giovanni who stood next to her, holding a glass of red wine. She smiled. "Yes...yes, it's me. I got a little hungry."

Actually, she wanted to run into the kitchen and ravage the place for anything and everything she could find. Food was all she could think of. Good food. Spicy Italian food.

"We've been waiting for you. Have some wine. Wine is good for the heart. Everybody needs a little wine," he said and handed her the glass.

What was it with these people and wine? She thought they were all trying to turn her into some sort of alcoholic.

She took the glass, smiled and immediately thought about the company directive that forbade drinking while on the job. She wanted to tell the whole group they were a disgrace to B-Logic. Demand they return to Subito right now, and work through the night to get the chip out.

But she didn't.

Instead, she drank down the entire glass of wine, an amazingly smooth Chianti, and let out a contented sigh.

"We just ordered," Rosalyn said, "but there's plenty for everyone. They serve everything family style here. It's like being at home."

Home, Lucy thought. There's no place like home. She wished she were there that very moment, after she ate something, of course.

"I just want a salad," Lucy told her, trying for some self-control while Giovanni refilled her glass.

"You only think you do. Wait till you see what we've ordered. You'll change your mind."

"I can't. My pants won't zip."

"You're not fat until the day you step into the shower and look down and can't see your..." Rosalyn whispered, reaching for a crust of bread.

"Is that your fat meter?"

Lucy sipped her wine. This time it was a fragrant merlot. She could totally recognize the difference and for an instant, she felt as though that was a significant accomplishment.

"Yep! I never have to get on a scale. All I have to do is look down. If I can't see it, I don't eat..."

Lucy choked a little on her wine, but managed to control herself rather quickly. There would be no choking in front of her fellow co-workers.

"Are you all right?" Rosalyn asked.

"Yes," Lucy said, but she was still coughing.

Finally, after a drink of water, she gained control of her throat.

"Don't worry so much," Rosalyn said. "You'll lose anything you gain when you go back home. Just have fun. You're on a company-paid vacation! We'll go shopping tomorrow at that cool shop I told you about. They've got some really great expandable skirts. You'll love it."

Lucy couldn't understand why everyone thought this was some kind of vacation. It was work. She'd been sent here to do a job which usually she was very good at. Granted, she hadn't gotten off to a very good start, but that was this morning. Tonight, well, this afternoon, had been great. Right on track. She was sick of everyone's "relax-baby" attitude.

She drank down her glass of wine and poured another from the endless supply of bottles in the middle of the table. She recognized a few of them from that morning in Frascati, but didn't dwell on the coincidence. Among the mix were some regional wines: Aglianico, Taurasi and Lacryma Cristi, the tears of Christ. She remembered these wines from her parents' table.

Two extremely cute waiters, who flirted with the women at the table, including Lucy, served the first course in large white tureens. Rosalyn had been right. Lucy took one look at the *pomodoro* soup and filled her bowl. When the *insalata* arrived with pears, roasted pecans and prosciutto on large yellow platters, Lucy was the first one to slip a mound on her plate. The glass of white wine that someone had poured her went down too quickly. She was getting drunk and didn't particularly want that to happen again, especially in front of her co-workers, so she sat back to watch for a while and take a wine-drinking rest.

They were singing, dancing, laughing and generally having a great time. Isabella and her husband, Mario, were there, sitting at the far end of the table, talking, kissing, having fun.

It was a work-night and this group of engineers was just getting started. Even Mr. Blue Socks, who sat at the other end of the table, was laughing over something that Debra had obviously just said. He was leaning in.

This jovial picture would have to change if they were ever going to make that tape-out date. She thought she should stand up and say something, make a company announcement, but the fish course arrived, and Lucy didn't want to be rude. Giovanni would hate her if she said anything negative when fish was being served.

After ingesting as much delicate white fish—smothered in bits of tomatoes and large black olives in a creamy white-wine sauce—as she could possibly fit inside her ever-expanding stomach, she turned to Rosalyn and said in a rather loud voice, "Whoever prepared this meal has to be fabulous in bed."

"He is," Rosalyn said, taking another bite of fish and moaning over the flavor. "Amazing!"

"You slept with the chef?"

"Only once, but it was definitely memorable. The things that man can do with olive oil are incredible!"

Lucy coughed and gulped down some water. Rosalyn patted her on the back. Lucy was going to have to get used to this woman or die coughing.

When her throat cleared, she said, "Olive oil?"

"Mmm," Rosalyn said and nodded, then she whispered. "There's something absolutely delicious about making it with a chef. They know precisely what it takes to get a woman off. Must have something to do with the way they cook, a pinch of this, a touch of that, all that tasting."

Lucy stared at her, wine glass in midair. All she wanted was one lousy orgasm and this girl had had it all and more. What was that all about?

"Are you two still together?"

"No. I'm way over him, but the things he can do to a woman should be illegal, probably are in some states. It's a good thing he lives in *Napoli*. Sex and lovemaking are national pastimes here. *La dolce vita* isn't just a term. It's a way of life." She looked over Lucy's shoulder and smirked. "You want me to introduce you? He just walked out of the kitchen."

"Me? No. Not me. I'm getting married on Saturday."

"That's Saturday's problem. This is Monday. You're still a free agent."

Rosalyn had a definite way with words.

"No. I love my fiancé."

"Then why are you here?" a sensual voice uttered right behind her left ear.

She could feel his hot breath on her neck. It gave her an instant rush of adrenaline.

Lucy turned around to see Vittorio sitting in the chair next to her, wearing a chef's white jacket.

She glanced back to Rosalyn.

Rosalyn gave her a sly little smile and a nod.

But Lucy had walked away from this man just that morning. He was the one man she never wanted to see again. Had promised herself she would never see again. The man she thought she had gotten rid of, forever.

Vittorio was the pincher? The olive-oil lover?

And, unfortunately, the chef next door.

"You two know each other?" Rosalyn asked.

"I wouldn't go that far," Lucy said. "We met on the plane."

"Ah, Lucia. I think we know each other pretty good," he said and took her hand to kiss it.

"Don't...don't do that." She pulled her hand away. "Why didn't you tell me you worked here?"

"He's the owner," Rosalyn said. "The keeper of the company tab."

"You own this place?"

He smiled, looked around and shrugged.

"Why didn't you tell me?"

"I try, but you were, how do I say? You were concerned with other things this morning."

Rosalyn picked up on the "this morning" part. "You were with Vittorio this morning?" Rosalyn turned to Lucy and said, "You devil, you."

"It's not what you think. It was a simple ride to Naples. That's all." The noise level increased, Rosalyn moved in to listen. "I couldn't rent...he offered...we made all these stops...then at the Santa Maria...well, I must have fallen, or we must have fallen."

"You fell?" Rosalyn asked, yelling over the din.

"No. What I meant was we must have fallen asleep." But Rosalyn still wasn't getting it.

"Asleep," Lucy repeated.

No response.

Then the room quieted for a moment, and in that brief span of unrecognized silence, Lucy, consumed with all the day's frustrations, blurted out in her clearest, loudest tones, "We slept together! Vittorio and I slept together."

Everyone at the table looked at Lucy. Everyone in the entire restaurant looked at Lucy. And as far as Lucy was concerned, everyone in Naples, in Italy, in the entire world looked at Lucy.

She wanted just to die right there.

Vittorio grinned while Lucy tried to explain the details of her morning, but somewhere during Lucy's muddled tale, Giovanni held up his glass and said, "To Lucia. To Vittorio. *La dolce vita!*" The entire table joined in on the toast as Lucy watched her credibility disappear with a gulp of red wine.

# 9

LUCY SLITHERED OUT of the restaurant as soon as she could convince Rosalyn, and anybody else who would listen, that she really, honestly, absolutely had not slept with Vittorio. At least not *that* way.

Vittorio was no help with the convincing. He simply grinned, shrugged a couple times, ordered another bottle of wine for the table, and disappeared into the kitchen, leaving Lucy to explain her outburst.

Which she eventually gave up on.

No one actually cared.

By the time she was out on the sidewalk, dragging her suitcase, Lucy was so brain-tired that she followed behind Rosalyn never saying a word for the entire walk home.

As they walked on the narrow sidewalk of the up-scale, all-dressed-up part of Naples with modern store-fronts and way-cool nightclubs, ahead of them a young couple kissed while leaning on a light post. His lips never left hers. Their arms were wrapped tightly around each other.

They kissed as Lucy and Rosalyn approached.

They kissed as Lucy and Rosalyn passed them by.

They kissed during the many times that Lucy turned to check them out.

And they kissed as Lucy and Rosalyn turned the cor-ner toward Rosalyn's flat. It amazed her that one kiss could last that long, be that passionate, exude such emotion. She had forgotten that public kissing was an honored tradition in Naples, and she thought about kissing Seth for that long.

He'd probably fall asleep.

Rosalyn's flat was on the second floor over an apparently very popular night club. The music, including the vocals, could be heard everywhere inside the building, and most especially inside Rosalyn's itty-bitty apartment. "Isn't this awesome?" Rosalyn said standing in the middle of what appeared to be a living room-kitchen combo.

"Awesome," Lucy sighed as she looked around for a bedroom. She didn't see one right off, just a curtain hanging across a large doorway, but it was dark in the room. All she really wanted at that exact moment was to fall into bed, pull the covers over her head and make the world stop...just for a few hours. Just until morning.

"You can have the bed. I usually sleep behind that curtain on the floor so I can feel the beat. It rocks me to sleep at night."

The bed she referred to was a queen-size futon, covered in layers of sixties-colored blankets lying on the floor next to a wall. A sleepy tabby cat opened one eye to take a peek at the intruders, then closed it again obviously secure in what he or she saw.

Lucy was not amused.

"Is that yours?" Lucy asked, pointing to the furry ball.

"Not exactly. That's Andrew. He's his own cat. Came with the apartment."

"I'm allergic to cats. They make me sneeze."

"You're not sneezing now."

"Give me time."

"No one's allergic to Andrew. He's part human. I think he was once a Caesar."

"Well, that's different then, isn't it?" Lucy sneezed. "I thought when you said your roommate was gone, you were offering me her bedroom, not her futon in the living room."

"Whatever gave you that idea? Like I could afford a real apartment in *Napoli*."

"Silly me," Lucy said dropping her things on the floor to search her purse for a tissue. She came up with one and blew her nose.

"I can hardly afford this flat on what I make. It's either hot clothes or a traditional place to live. I chose the clothes. A girl has to stick to her priorities or what else is there?"

It made perfect sense for Rosalyn's world. "You're right," she sneezed. "Priorities."

"You're so cool. Anyway, this is a one-room flat. There are no actual bedrooms."

"Is there a bathroom, or do I have to use the sink?"

Lucy's nose really bugged her now. The cat would have to go, or go under something if she was ever going to get some sleep. And what she wanted more than her next breath, was sleep. Actual, honest-to-God sleep.

"That's disgusting. Of course there's a bathroom," Rosalyn said and walked over to what had to be the best thing Lucy had seen since she'd arrived in this overcrowded, noisy, most definitely confusing city. "The other reason why I took this place."

Rosalyn opened an actual door and inside, painted muted shades of grays and blues, with a clean white tile floor, was a luxurious, spacious bathroom. A retreat of sorts, with a chaise lounge next to a brown-and-orange beaded curtain that hid a huge, round, sunken bathtub.

Heaven.

"It's beautiful." Lucy couldn't believe her tired eyes. The fancy tub was just what she needed to soothe the day away. Okay, so Rosalyn wasn't so bad, after all.

"Have fun," Rosalyn said.

"Thanks. I will," she answered, smiling at the prospect of a hot bath with bubbles and real soap.

Abruptly, Rosalyn turned and left the flat.

Lucy was finally alone in a room of her own, or at least a-room-of-her-own-for-now, and for now it was enough.

Except for the critter staring up at her from the futon.

Andrew would have to go, or at least Lucy tried to get him to go, but he wouldn't budge when she did her usual "shoo, shoo" sounds to scare him off. It worked on other cats, why not Andrew?

Nope, Andrew just stared at her as though she was a pesky gnat, then got up, stretched and curled up on the foot of the futon. At least he was out of her way.

She sneezed again. Her phone rang. It was her mother.

"You could be dead and I wouldn't know," she said.

"If I were dead, you'd know. Something would itch or burn."

"Why haven't you called me?"

"I've been busy. Sorry."

"Busy with what? You leave me here to plan your wedding and you're too busy! What do you know from busy? I got a chef here who can't cook Italian food and a florist who can't find pink hydrangeas this time of year. How you gonna have a nice Italian wedding without fried sausage and hydrangeas?"

"I didn't know I was having an Italian wedding."

"What other kind of wedding is there?"

"A simple one."

"Nothing's simple in this life, Lucia. Don't you know that yet?"

Lucy could feel the tension mounting.

"I'm beginning to. Is Seth helping you?"

"Seth is busy with Seth."

"What does that mean?"

"It means he ordered that horrible fountain. I don't agree with it, but what am I gonna say? I'm only the mother. So, are you coming home tomorrow?"

"I won't be home until Friday night. You already know that."

"If you don't come home tomorrow, you won't come home on Friday."

"Why do you say these things?"

"Because I know life."

"You know *your* life."

"You're my daughter. I know your life. Did you meet him yet?"

Lucy's breath caught in her throat. How could she know? "Who?"

"The Donico son. Why do you always forget what I tell you to do?"

"Mom, Naples is a big city. How am I supposed to find someone named 'the Donico son'? Do you know how many Donicos there are in Naples?"

"No, do you?"

"Mom, please stop."

She thought about a means of escape. She would have to adjust to the madness.

"That's my job."

"To drive me crazy? I thought it was to nurture and guide me?"

"That's your father's job. Mine is to give you life and make sure you're happy."

"How can I be happy if you're driving me crazy?"

"Because I force you to think about sausage and hydrangeas."

"I have to go, Ma. I love you."

"I love you too. Rest good tonight and know that your mother has the wedding with what's-his-name under control, even though I know you won't be there."

"Mom!"

"*Buono note*, Lucia."

"*Buono note*, Mom."

Lucy let out a sigh, snapped her phone shut and looked around for an outlet. When she found one, she plugged in her adaptor, dragged the cord up to the futon and set up her cell in its charger. She found a clean set of sheets in a hidden closet next to the sink in the bathroom and made up the futon in bright purples. There were clean towels for her bath, and an ivory-colored bar of French soap wrapped in tissue sitting on a shelf next to the beaded door. She took her pj's and hung them on a silver hook. No matter what else was whacked in her life, she was determined to enjoy this moment of solitude.

As the tub filled with water, she added a stream of bubble bath to the flow and for some reason got into the music vibrating under her feet. She danced to the rhythm. If she was going to have to live with the music she might as well enjoy it. She tried to toss everything out of her head and just go with the beat as it vibrated the floor and walls of the tiny flat. For a moment, she could forget about her mother, the wedding, Seth, Subito and Vittorio. She twirled and danced, caught up in the rhythm until she was out of breath and sweaty. Each movement made her happy, made her laugh as she slid across the floor in her socks, and gyrated her hips for a totally uninhibited feeling. She removed her blouse and flung it across the room, then her slacks. Her head swung back and forth, hair loose and swaying. The feeling, incredible.

When the song ended, she eagerly shed her underwear and stepped into the now completely full tub, content with the world. But as soon as she settled into the bubbly water, Vittorio slipped into her consciousness like the scent of roses in a garden, ever-present, strong, lustful.

She took the bar of soap into her hands and rolled it over and over, feeling its silky cream spread. Then she washed herself gently with the lather, first her neck, the front, up the sides, the back.

She pulled her hair up, and fastened it with a long silver clip sitting beside the tub. Then she lathered her hands again and washed her breasts, each one, with long, firm motions, pulling at the nipples. She thought of Vittorio's hands, those long fingers resting on the stick shift of his Alfa Romeo.

She let out a small yelp when her phone rang.

She ignored it.

It stopped.

She slid further down into the tub. Her phone rang again. Obviously, someone wanted to talk to her. Maybe it was Seth wanting to wish her a loving goodnight, or her mother wanting to ask her some question about the wedding, or maybe, somehow, it was Vittorio.

She had to answer.

She got out of the tub, grabbed a small towel and raced across the room, dropping soapsuds as she went. Her feet slid on the linoleum floor as she grabbed for support wherever she could, until she took one final step and somehow landed face down on the futon, right next to Andrew. Slowly, she turned to face him. He picked up his head, licked her nose and looked at her.

Yuk!

She sneezed and answered the phone. "Hello," she sneezed again.

It was her boss, Dennis. "Hope you're not catching a cold there. We need you to be on top of things! Take some Cold Ease. You'll be fine in twenty-four hours. Miracle drug. We're in the middle of a status meeting and need your input. I know it's late there, but I also know that you're probably at work right now, although no one answered when I called the main number. But that's probably because you've got everyone working so hard they don't have time to answer the phone. Is that it?"

She sneezed. She sneezed again. And again. Andrew jumped off the futon and onto a chair. He stared down at her with his big golden eyes.

"That's it!" she said, giving them what they wanted to hear.

"Good, that's great news. Around the clock. That's what we need. Keep after 'em, Lucy. You have our complete support. Whatever it takes." It was another engineer talking. A smarmy little guy with bad breath. His squeaky voice reminded her that she was naked, covered in soapsuds, lying on a futon in the middle of a strange room talking to her co-workers.

She couldn't breathe. Her chest felt tight and her hands, clammy. If she wasn't already lying down, she would probably have collapsed from the sudden lack of oxygen.

Was there no place sacred?

She hated her cell phone.

"So, will we make our tape-out date on Friday? We're depending on you," Dennis said. "This is make-or-break-it time for Subito. If they don't make it, I'm afraid, as a company, we'll have to reallocate the resources. So, what's it going to be?"

"You got it. The S9293 will go out on time," she said, trying to sound normal. Pulling short bursts of air into her ever-constricting lungs.

She positively, absolutely had no idea when the chip from hell would be ready...and what was this new thing about reallocating resources? These were people, not minerals.

The music started up again, a really loud song. Lucy tried to cover the receiver.

"Sounds like you're in a nightclub," Dennis said. She could hear everyone chuckle.

"No. They just like to work to music around here," she said. Andrew let out a loud meow, and jumped back on the futon right next to her.

"Was that a cat?" Dennis asked.

Lucy had to think fast. "I can't hear you very well," her voice got louder as Andrew droned on. "What did you say?"

"I said, do you have a cat there?"

"Sorry, I'm going to have to go. The connection's bad. Oh, and don't call the work phone for a while.

We're too busy to answer. I'll send you an e-mail in the morning with the status. Bye."

She snapped her phone shut and started sneezing, over and over again while Andrew cried over and over again. She found the blankets next to the bed and pulled them up over her, covering even her head. She attempted the cleansing breath strategy, and somehow, with the music pushing up through the floor, and Andrew's constant whine, she drifted off to sleep.

# 10

LAUGHTER AWOKE her sometime well into the early morning, four-fifty-three to be exact. At first, she didn't know where she was, but when Andrew stepped on her stomach to give her a loud greeting, she remembered every detail. She pushed him off and sat up. At once she was cold. Freezing, actually. The front window was wide open. She wrapped the blanket around her until she could find her pajamas, which she hoped were still hanging on the hook in the bathroom.

Great place for them, she thought.

The miserable phone call with Dennis and her co-workers came rushing into her brain. That's why she was naked. At least she could piece everything back together.

She found her pj's right where she had left them. Things were looking up. She could actually remember stuff if she didn't drink too much. "What a concept," she said out loud.

Once wrapped in Old Navy comfort, she went in search of the voices. They seemed to be coming from outside, from the street below.

Lucy went to the front window to get a look, yawning as she went, wondering why these people didn't seem to need sleep. And on a work night! Andrew followed, jumping up on the sill to get his own look at the sleep invaders.

There was a full moon in the sky and with the help of some pretty worthless streetlights she could make out the people milling around below.

Lucy let out another yawn as she peered at the mix of characters, laughing, talking, kissing. A couple leaned on the building across the way engrossed in another Neapolitan endless kiss. She couldn't take her eyes off them. His arms completely encircled the girl. It was like watching Tom Selleck in an old episode of *Magnum P.I.* He'd engulf his latest quest in his embrace. Her mother was a big fan. It was one of those shows the two of them had never missed. A moment in time when she and her mother could agree on something—Tom Selleck rocked! Back then, Lucy had thought that when she grew up she would find someone just like him, someone who held a woman as though she was the most important person in his life, even if it was for only an hour every Monday night on prime-time television. She'd believed she would find someone in the real world just like him.

Lucy wanted to be held like that, kissed like that—completely enveloped by her lover.

Maybe she could teach Seth. Make him watch reruns of *Magnum, P.I.* Practice embraces while they watched the sun set.

Could happen. She sighed.

Andrew meowed and yawned.

Lucy watched the lovers as she daydreamed of passionate moments and sensual hugs, moonlight and romance, lovemaking and king-size beds with satin sheets. She rubbed her arms to keep warm, to ward off the night chill, when suddenly the kissing couple let go of their embrace and walked under the streetlight.

It was Rosalyn, and the guy looked a lot like Vittorio. Was it Vittorio? How could she? How could he?

Lucy leaned out of the window to get a better look, but it was too dark outside and even with the street-light she couldn't see. Not really. All she knew was they weren't heading back into the club, they were heading into the doorway for this apartment.

She ran to the futon and covered her head with the blanket. After a moment, she could hear them coming up the stairs together, talking loudly and laughing even louder. The nerve! She felt betrayed by a girl she had just met and a man who made her angry whenever he opened his mouth to speak.

The key turned in the lock. She waited, barely breathing. What would she do if they started making out right there in the living room? Would she sit up and tell them to find some other place to do their kissing? Or would she just throw something at them, maybe the cat.

She fantasized about Andrew landing on Vittorio's back, clawing his way down, blood oozing from between his sharp little nails. The look on Vittorio's face when she snapped on the light.

What would he say? How would he react to her presence? The little boy-slut.

"He's not even that cute," she mumbled out loud.

She wondered how he got all these girls to drop their pants when they knew he was nothing but a flirt, a ship looking for a port. And it didn't seem to matter whose port. Not that she wanted it to be hers, but Rosalyn had said she was "way over him." And what exactly did *way* mean in Rosalyn's dictionary of hip terms?

Way: a temporary gap in time.
Way: a moment of forgetfulness.
Way: a second before you change your mind.

Whatever it was, when the door opened, Lucy lay dead still and waited as Rosalyn and Vittorio dropped "way" into the trash and brought themselves back to "now."

"Shh," Rosalyn whispered as she and Vittorio walked by her futon. Lucy was seething, shaking with anger, sure they could see the blanket tremble from the sheer force of the pounding of her heart. Fine, she thought, they're going to do it behind that nasty curtain. Shit-shit-shit!

Andrew leaped off the futon. "Hi sweetheart," Rosalyn said as Andrew cried for her attention. "Are you hungry, baby? I bet she didn't feed you, huh?"

*Feed him!* Lucy thought. Like, she even knew to feed the cat. Like, she had done something wrong by not feeding the cat. How was she supposed to know about cats?

Remorse swept over her. So now she felt both guilt and anger. She hated Naples, hated Andrew, Rosalyn and most especially hated Vittorio who was probably standing over her right now, stripping.

"You can wait for me behind the curtain. I'll just be a minute," Rosalyn cooed.

Lucy could hear footsteps trail off as an electric can opener whirled. Moments later, Rosalyn followed across the tile floor. Then the loud laughter started up again.

Lucy couldn't stand it. Couldn't stand the fun of it, the foreplay of it. They kept getting louder and louder as Rosalyn's voice got lower and lower.

Okay, so she'd put the pillow over her head and pretend the TV was on. They weren't real, just shadows in a box. And why did she care? She was getting married on Saturday…this Saturday, to a great guy. A guy who loved her, adored her, worshiped her ground, or something like that. Okay, so maybe he didn't worship, but he loved her, or at least he said he did. Sometimes…during Friday-night sex.

Well, maybe not as much as he loved electronics or his own buffed body, but love wasn't all it was cracked up to be, anyway.

Who cared about love? Not her. There were more important things in life besides love.

Weren't there?

She couldn't answer the question because she was too busy concentrating on Vittorio's voice coming from the bedroom, sexy and low. She couldn't make out what he was saying, but whatever it was, she couldn't stand it anymore. She had to tell them to keep it down. Let them know she was awake. She didn't want to hear Rosalyn's no doubt multiple orgasms. Didn't want to know the details of certain pinching.

Lucy threw the blankets off and marched to the curtain, stomping her feet as she went for effect.

But the voices didn't stop. "Oooh, right there," Rosalyn sighed.

Lucy banged on the wall next to the curtain, her fist throbbing from the force, her nails pinching the soft flesh of her hand.

Silence.

She banged again, only this time the curtain swung open in the middle of her tirade, and there, standing in front of her, bare-chested, wearing bright red boxers, was a drop-dead gorgeous, fabulously built…complete stranger.

He smiled.

"It's not you," she blurted out, entirely embarrassed. Rosalyn lay half-naked on the bed, waving her fingers, smiling. "Did you need something?" she asked, grinning.

Lucy felt as if everyone in the entire world could see what an absolute ass she had just made of herself. She couldn't speak. Couldn't move. She merely stood there with her arm still up in the air like a Barbie some little girl had just manipulated into a dumb position. It was as though she had lost all control over her own body and was waiting for the little girl to move her arm back down.

Drop-dead-gorgeous spoke in Russian or something, pulled the curtain open all the way, and took a step back.

Rosalyn said, "I think he wants you to come join us."

Lucy rewound her brain, shook her head and cleared away all thoughts of Vittorio. How could she have been so wrong-headed? "No. Thanks," she said. "Not my thing, but you two go ahead. Have fun. I'll just go back out to my futon. It's right out there. In the living room...way over there."

Lucy let her arm fall to her side, spun around and calmly walked back to her pseudo-bed.

Andrew sat in the middle of it, licking his paws then wiping his ears and his face, completely oblivious to what had just happened.

The curtain closed. Rosalyn and her latest quest started up again. Lucy slid under the covers on the futon. Andrew got up, took a couple steps forward, turned around and sat down right next to her face. He then proceeded to stare at her, making her feel even more like an ass.

She sneezed into her pillow five times in a row. When she looked up he was still there, watching, golden eyes wide with wonder, as if he were trying to figure her out.

"Don't you have anything better to do?" she asked.

Andrew let out a little meow and went back to his cleaning.

# 11

"IT DOESN'T MEAN anything," Rosalyn said.

"It's got to mean something. How could I be jealous?" Lucy had locked herself in the bathroom, but Rosalyn had convinced Lucy to let her in. The Russian lay sleeping, for the moment. Rosalyn, dressed in a red silk robe, sat in the chaise while Lucy paced the bathroom floor.

"It happens to me all the time," Rosalyn said, stretching out on the chair.

"Yes, but I don't actually think that's normal."

"Define normal."

"You know what I mean."

"Lucy, don't overreact to your overreaction."

"You're not making sense."

"Okay, what's the problem?" Rosalyn asked. "Shouldn't you be sleeping or something? Don't you have a meeting in the morning?"

"I can't sleep. This is critical!"

"Let's see if I have it. You're jealous over a guy who's doing it with me, who you've just met, because you thought the guy was Vittorio, who you also just met and are attracted to and say you didn't actually have sex with—too bad—only Vittorio makes you nuts. And you're tormented by this because you're getting married in a few days."

"Something like that."

"Catholic guilt. You must have been taught by nuns."

"Well, yes, but...what?"

"Your Catholic guilt is showing. It's because of the Pope."

"What does the Pope have to do with this?"

"He lives down the street."

"He lives in Rome."

"Whatever. The Man is too close. He's guilting you."

"Guilting me? What's that supposed to mean?"

"It's like thinking about sex inside a confessional. Way too creepy. You need perspective."

"Okay, give me some."

"What?"

"Perspective. Give me some perspective."

"I can't right now. My Russian god is leaving for a gig in Como in a few hours and he promised to show me how Dr. Guang Yue's new fitness theory works. It's all in your mind."

"Perspective?"

"No. Fitness. This doctor has proven you can increase the strength of your pinkie by thirty-five percent just by thinking about it for fifteen minutes a day."

"And you have a need for stronger pinkies?"

"No, but think of the possibilities." Rosalyn got up, gave Lucy a hug and a kiss on her cheek and left.

Lucy continued to sit in the bathroom trying to get perspective. She thought perhaps Rosalyn was right, or was it Dr. Yue? Fitness, whether physical or emotional was all a matter of correct thinking.

She flexed her fingers and concentrated on stronger pinkies.

After a few minutes she flexed again. Her pinkies were definitely stronger.

SUBITO WAS already humming when Lucy got to work that morning. Granted, it was a little later than she had hoped to get in, ten-thirty, but she was back on track. She had somehow managed to sleep right through Rosalyn's departure, and drop-dead-gorgeous had left sometime just after dawn. Lucy had heard him say his goodbyes and slam the door shut. It was a blessing that Rosalyn wasn't sitting at her desk in the lobby when Lucy walked through. She just wanted to put all of yesterday out of her mind.

Okay, she was back at work now.

She shoved her purse in a drawer, and set up her laptop next to the Sun monitor on Frank's desk.

Hot. She was boiling because of the black suit she had decided to wear. She had wanted to wear something that said, "take me seriously," but all she'd managed to do was make herself sweat. She took off the jacket, rolled up the sleeves on her blouse, and clipped her hair up in a roll. She would have to let everything else go and concentrate on the chip. Her promotion to director of program managers, not to mention the destiny of this very office, depended on getting this project out on time. Everything rode on her ability to make it happen. Her personal problems just had to wait until later to be resolved.

First thing she had to do was order a vending machine, two vending machines, one for actual food and snacks and the other for coffee.

Not knowing where to order a vending machine, she would have to depend on Rosalyn. She picked up the phone, hoping by some miracle that Rosalyn was actually at her desk. Lucy thought of walking over there to talk to her personally, but she really didn't want to see the woman for a while. She had seen quite enough of her last night.

"Good morning, Lucy," Rosalyn said, all cheerful.

Her voice made Lucy cringe. "I want to have a couple vending machines installed. Today if possible. One for sandwiches and snacks and the other for coffee," Lucy announced with an edge to her voice. She didn't want any grief.

"Nobody will use them," Rosalyn answered, apparently unimpressed.

"I don't care what you think. Just do it."

"Like, get a grip. I didn't say I wouldn't."

"Fine and get rid of the tab next door." Lucy was on a management roll. She felt powerful. Mighty. Filled with authority. It was a good feeling.

"I can't do that unless Giovanni tells me to."

"I'm telling you to."

"He's my boss."

"I'm your boss today." This was getting good, a real honest-to-God subordinate problem. It was a heady experience and she liked it. So far, anyway.

"How long will you want the vending machines for?"

"For forever."

"That's a long time."

"Just do it," Lucy demanded and hung up. She felt like Captain Picard giving orders from the bridge. "Make it so," was all she needed to say and people would jump. Absolute power.

What a head-rush!

Next she had to get a status from Giovanni and send an e-mail to Dennis to confirm what she'd told him last night, even if she had to lie. Even if she had to stay there all night long and run the top-level rules herself, she would get that chip out so she could go home.

She told herself she would not think about Vittorio, or about food or sex until her goal was accomplished. No matter what it took.

Determined and self-assured, she tromped over to Giovanni's office, a large room just like Frank's and just as noisy, but decorated with pictures of Giovanni holding up various sized fish. When she entered his office, he sat with his back to her, facing his monitor, a schematic up on the screen. She knocked on his open door and waited.

"Giovanni, we need to talk," she said standing in front of his desk, her hands at her sides, chin up, chest out, Captain Picard in drag.

"Ah, Lucia. It's a good day to talk," he said all smiles, apparently not recognizing her authority, her importance.

"What's the status of the project?" she demanded, a curtness to her voice. This was getting easier by the minute. She was going to make one hell of a director.

"We have a final design review this morning. The team, we are happy. We have a few signals to shield, a few decoupling caps to add to the top, some power lines to make wider, a couple pad cells we need to change, a diode here, a diode there and we will be in business...that is if the server, she don't go down."

"What will it take to keep it up?"

"God's gotta like us," he said with a twinkle in his eye.

She didn't like his flippant attitude. Didn't he realize how important this chip was? How symbolically important it was to at least pretend that nothing like a server going down could possibly happen before tape-out? "Aside from an act of God, what will it actually take?"

"This is Italy. Sometime, the power, she goes out. Sometime, who knows. But you know how these things go. One minute you think you're going to make it and the next...pfsst...nothing. Everything stops." He shrugged.

"But, of course, you have someone on the team who can get the system up and running if it goes down?"

"Of course!"

"Good. I can help with the layout if you need me to. Whatever it takes."

"After lunch. You can add the decoupling caps on the top. Isabella, she can work on the LVS."

"That's fine. Just so you know, I took the liberty of ordering a couple vending machines."

"The liberty is yours."

"Then you don't mind?" This Picard thing was getting easier and easier. Lucy really liked the whole idea of it.

"Why should I mind?"

Relieved that she wouldn't have to fight her case, she relaxed a bit and sat down in a chair. This was getting too easy. "I also had Rosalyn close the tab next door."

"Only I can close the tab."

"But don't you agree that it's disruptive?"

"What is disruptive? Eating?"

"No, having a tab at a restaurant."

"You don't think we should eat?"

She clenched her teeth and stood up, thinking she had let her guard down by sitting. The power was in the standing, taking up room, dominating the space. She had learned the technique in *SWE* magazine.

"I didn't say you shouldn't eat. Of course, you

should eat. Everyone needs to. I try to eat something every day."

He smiled one of those what-are-you-trying-to-say-you-loser-girl smiles.

She wasn't making sense. She hated it when she didn't make sense. Taking a deep breath, she went on. Slowly. "What I mean is, the company shouldn't have to pay for everyone's morning espresso. And the company should most certainly not have to pay for everyone's dinner if no one returns to work after dinner."

"Why not?"

"Because it defeats the whole purpose."

"Of what?"

"Of a company-paid dinner!"

"Come," he said. "It's time for coffee. It would be the company's honor to buy such a hard-working woman like yourself an espresso."

Almost numb, she followed Giovanni out of his office like an obedient pet. What galled her the most was his total disregard for her Picard metamorphosis.

THE VENDING MACHINES arrived sooner than Lucy had expected, before lunch. Apparently, when there's profit involved, a vending-machine company can act pretty quickly. The machines were rather large, and when they were rolled into the lobby, they overpowered the small room so that Rosalyn had to move her desk back against the far wall, almost into the next office.

Okay, so vending machines in the lobby didn't look so hot sitting along the walls, humming like, well, like vending machines. Their sheer size was daunting, but in the long run they would save time, and that's what this was all about…time.

Lucy called a meeting.

"From now on," she said, still on her Picard kick, "or at least until this chip goes out, there will be no long lunches. As you know, there are now a couple of vending machines in the lobby for your convenience. They'll be stocked with an assortment of sandwiches, fresh fruit and other tasty treats."

Blue Socks asked, "Like what?"

He caught Lucy by surprise. She had no idea what kind of food Rosalyn had ordered. She thought of the kinds of things she would eat at B-Logic, all of which usually made her slightly ill. "Pasta. Sandwiches. Cheese and crackers and—"

"What kind of pasta comes out of a machine?" Joe S. asked.

"A good pasta. I mean, so it's not the best, but it's hot and fills your stomach."

"And this you call a 'tasty treat'?" Blue Socks mocked.

"Sometimes. Sometimes I do. You'd be surprised."

One of the Joes said, "I bet I would!"

Everyone laughed.

Lucy continued, thinking she'd try the I'm-on-your-side approach. "Look, guys, I'm not trying to be the bad guy here. I'm just trying to help you meet the deadline. We have to put in as many hours as we can stand in order to reach our goal. If it means eating inferior food for a few days, then so be it!" As the words left her lips, she thought of her father. She sounded just like him. Is this what it meant to be a manager? A director? An adult? To stand in front of a group of perfectly reasonable people and have everyone stare at you with hate in their eyes?

Oh well, she thought. It comes with being in charge.

Even Picard had his enemies. "Are there any questions?"

"How much do we have to pay for these tasty treats?" Blue Socks asked, sarcasm resonating in his voice.

Lucy had to think quickly. Had to inspire these people not to leave the building. "It's all free for the first week as a thank you from B-Logic for working so hard."

She waited, expecting a "that's terrific" to fly across the table, but it didn't fly. Not even a buzz.

Silence. Long, agonizing silence.

"Well," she said. "If there are no more questions, let's get back to work."

Once again the group left in a hurry. It was time for lunch and she was hoping they were all on their way to the machines, anxious to get at it. Anxious to down some tasty, free food and get right back to work. That's what would happen if they were in the States, so why shouldn't she expect the same from the Italian office?

Free food was, after all, free.

Lucy returned to her office. She immediately sent out an e-mail to Dennis praising the wonders of herself and the vending-machine transition. Totally full of herself, she then walked out of her office to check on the subordinates, who were, in fact, still going at it well into the lunch hour. Matter of fact, none of them had left their desks since the meeting. She, however, was feeling a bit hungry.

She took great pride in walking through the rooms, looking at the employees tap-tap-tapping away at their keyboards. Schematics, layouts or simulation results resonated up on their screens. Proud that she had finally come up with the perfect solution to her mission, proud that American work ethics were finally taking hold in this easygoing atmosphere, she stood straighter. Walked taller. Had a smile on her face.

Ah, it felt good to be queen.

"I'm just going over to get something out of the machine," she said to Debra when she looked up from her workstation.

"That's nice," Debra said. Of course, Lucy couldn't actually hear her, but she read her lips and smiled.

Ah, sweet authority, it was a heady thing. She flashed on a meeting from years ago when the CEO of B-Logic had just taken office. One of the engineers had questioned his authority on an issue. A VP simply said, "He's the CEO. He can do anything he wants."

No truer words, Lucy thought with delight. This was it. She was on her way. If this had been a test, she had passed with an A-plus. Dad would be proud.

Totally at peace with herself, she turned the corner and entered the lobby.

Vittorio was just coming in through the front door carrying a large red bag. The kind of bag a caterer carried in the States. The kind of bag that usually contained hot restaurant food. Two waiters from his restaurant followed him in with more red bags. Lucy recognized one of them from the other night. He winked at her. She threw him a scowl. He winked again. Obviously, he didn't recognize authority when he saw it.

"You can set everything up here," Rosalyn told him and directed them to her desk and a long folding table extending from one side. The table was covered in white linen with stacks of fresh fruit on one side and silver chafing dishes in the middle.

"What's this?" Lucy asked, but no one seemed to

hear her. She repeated herself. "Excuse me, but what's going on?"

Vittorio looked up. "Ah, Lucia. We bring lunch." He kissed the tips of his bunched-up fingers. *"Delizioso!"*

"Don't you *delizioso* me. I know your game. *I* brought in lunch. It's right there in those machines. It's free."

Vittorio continued with his mission, ignoring her and unloading his bag. "That is not lunch. That is plastic. This is a meal." He held up a large bowl of linguini in a delicate red sauce with huge shrimp, tomatoes and olives. It looked positively fabulous, but Lucy ignored it.

"No. No. No. You can't do this. B-Logic bought everything in those machines. It's entirely free to the employees."

"And B-Logic buy this too. It's a good company this B-Logic. Yes?"

"No! I didn't buy your food. I bought the vending machine food. You can't do this. Take it back."

"I cannot do that."

"Yes you can. Just wrap it up in your little red cases and take it back."

"Why you want to make a big deal all the time? It will upset your stomach and you won't be able to enjoy your meal. Not good for your digestion to get upset."

"I don't want to enjoy my meal. I want to work. I'll enjoy my meal when I retire at sixty-something."

"But then you will be too old, and the taste in your tongue will be gone. Now is the time to enjoy your taste, not when you are old, with no taste."

She wanted both to laugh at what he had just said and yell at him for bringing in the food, but before she knew it, the entire staff was out in the lobby with forks in hand loading everything from antipasto to lobster ravioli with poppy-seed sauce, to baked sea bass with pine nuts on their white ceramic plates. He had even brought over dessert, a chocolate ricotta tart, and some kind of fresh mixed-berry, whipped-cream, yellow-cake thing that sat at the end of the table in a clear bowl.

Rosalyn busied herself uncorking various red wines. Lucy gave up with the food and moved her attention to Rosalyn, who was in direct conflict with company policy. "Wine. There's wine in the building? There's no drinking on company premises," Lucy ordered in a loud voice, completely losing her cool.

"But we cannot eat without a little wine. Just as you cannot eat without a Coke or an iced tea," Giovanni said. Everyone in the room chuckled. He had said it with an American accent.

Completely losing it, she said, "Whoever drinks that wine will lose their job. Right here. Right now."

"Lucia," Giovanni said, trying to reason with her. "You joke."

Lucy stood in front of the vending machines, one on either side, almost as if they were her bodyguards, her protectors. The employees stood in front of the food table, plates in hand, looking at her as if she had gone mad.

"I'm completely serious," she said, shaking with conviction. "I have the authority." She wasn't actually sure she really had the authority to fire someone, but it had gone way (and there was that word again) past reason. Everyone stared at her. Waiting. Deciding.

A stand-off between American vending-machine madness and European tradition. Which would win?

Lucy stood her ground.

The employees stood their ground, until Giovanni motioned to Rosalyn to back off the wine. Rosalyn put the corkscrew down on her desk.

Then, one by one, the team went back to their desks, in silence, without the wine, but with Vittorio's catered lunch.

"Lucia, you have made a big mistake," Vittorio said, solemnly.

"No," she said. "They have."

She turned triumphantly and pressed the button on the Coke machine. It made an awful noise, and, with one masterful move, red can after red can came tumbling out of the machine and bounced onto the floor. There was a crackling sound, a pop, the lights flickered, then everything went dark.

# 12

THERE'S A weird silence when the power goes down inside a once-busy office. The incessant humming stops. All those computers stop computing and the white-noise factor drops to zero. It's almost eerie, Lucy thought as she sat in the empty office.

She couldn't believe everyone had left the building after she had told them to stay.

Total insubordination!

So, okay, the lights went out because the vending machines pulled in too much power and something blew. But someone from the power company had come out and fixed it.

So then the phones went dead because of some kind of power surge, but someone from the phone company came out and fixed it.

Some of the systems finally came back up again, but she couldn't get into the project because the servers were hosed.

Okay fine, somebody would simply have to come back into work and take care of it, she thought.

There was nothing for her to do but wait. They had to return at some point. Didn't they?

Did they have no shame?

No guilt?

At least the phones worked. She put her head down on Frank's desk and sighed. Did everyone just play hooky whenever they wanted to? Was there no seriousness left in the world?

She dialed her mother.

"Mom?"

"What's wrong now?"

"It's me."

"I know it's you."

"Does something have to be wrong for me to call you?"

"No, but that's what you usually do."

"Let's not get into this."

"You're the one who called. I haven't even had my first cup of coffee yet. It's still dark outside, for pity's sake. How can I solve your problem without a cup of coffee?"

"Go get your coffee, Mom, I'll wait."

"Who's dime is this?"

"The company's."

"Okay, you can wait."

Her mother put the phone down. Lucy waited, thinking that she should never have phoned her mother. Thinking that her mother was a crazy-maker and by the end of the conversation she would have to take a pill. Her stomach started to ache just thinking about it.

She was just about to hang up when her mother came back on the line. "Now I can think and solve. What's up?"

"Did I ever play hooky from school when I was a kid?"

"You call me before I have my coffee for that? I thought it was going to be something terrible, and all you want to know is if you ever played hooky?"

"Yes. It's important."

"Why is this sooo important? You having childhood regrets? You don't like the way your father and me raised you?"

"Mom, no. I mean you did a fine job raising me. I was just wondering if we ever took a day off, you and me, to have fun?"

She could hear her mother slurping up the coffee. It must have been hot because her mother made little blowing sounds. Lucy pictured her mom sitting at the kitchen table, favorite Pier One cup and saucer in hand, blowing, sipping, thinking.

Her mom loved a good strong cup of coffee in the morning. Italian coffee. She would buy it by the pound from an Italian deli near the house. Lucy could never drink it, too bitter-tasting and too much caffeine.

"I remember one day. You must have been in fifth grade. You were so tired when I woke you up for school, poor thing. You wanted to know how many more days you would have to go."

She paused for a sip of coffee. Then went on.

"I told you it would be a very long time, and you started to cry. It broke my heart to see you cry like that, so we played hooky. Didn't tell your father, and we went to see an Indiana Jones movie at the movie theater. Twice. We got ice cream, went shopping and bought you a whole box of them Garbage Pail Kids trading cards. You were into those then. Remember?"

She flashed on her cards. She and her friends would sit for hours laughing over them while they sat up in the big tree out on her front lawn. Those cards were the best. Her mom would always buy a pack when she went grocery shopping. Her dad would throw them out whenever he found them lying around. Said they were ruining her intelligent brain.

Suddenly, Lucy hungered for just one card.

"Do I still have any?"

"Probably in a box somewhere. Why, you want me to send you some?"

Lucy sat up straight. "Of course not. I just wanted to know if they were around."

"So, you called me to ask about a set of kids' cards?"

"I guess so."

"Okay. You give me a call if you need more advice."

"But you didn't give me any advice."

"Sure I did. Love you." And she hung up.

Lucy hung up, then she put her head back down on Frank's desk and let out a long, loud sigh....

*Lucy sits at a large metal desk, typing numbers into a computer, endless streams of numbers with no meaning. She's in a large corner office with a view of Silicon Valley. Shiny computer chips, the size of coasters, clutter her desk. Everything, including her skin, has a blue tinge to it. A plastic kitchen timer goes off on the desk. She looks at her watch, gets up, and takes a Starbuck's paper coffee cup out of the blue microwave that sits on top of a blue filing cabinet. The coffee cup has a rubber nipple sticking out of the top. She slides open the top drawer of the cabinet and there's a baby inside looking up at her, smiling, all pink and happy. She smiles down on the perfect little bundle and hands it the coffee cup. The baby grabs it and begins to suckle. Lucy watches for a moment until another timer goes off somewhere in the distance. She slides the drawer shut and goes back to the endless stream of numbers.*

WHEN LUCY awoke from her disturbing dream, she found herself sitting on the floor next to a black filing cabinet in the corner of the room. She heard a noise out in the other part of the office and immediately jumped back into Frank's uncomfortable green chair. She couldn't take any more ridicule.

When·no one appeared in her doorway, she decided to check on the noise. It was Giovanni. He had come in to check up on things. He knew nothing about hard drives, but he had a second sense about him that Lucy thought was freaky. How he knew that some of the systems were humming again was beyond her.

He informed her that he had contacted Frank, the Colombian hostage. Lucy couldn't quite recall the relevance, but was somewhat glad to hear that Frank was indeed all right.

"So we lost a few hours, six to be exact, because of the power thing, but once the servers are back on-line everything will be fine," she told Giovanni who was busy reading his e-mail. She stood in his office, in front of his desk.

"That is correct," he said, continuing to read and type.

"So, where's this I.T. person?" Lucy couldn't believe he wouldn't even give her the courtesy of looking up.

"In Colombia," he said.

Lucy didn't get it for a moment, then it all came rushing back.

"Frank? Frank's I.T?"

"Yes."

"But Frank's been kidnapped."

"Yes, that was unfortunate, but it sometimes happens. Like I said, he's at home now."

"In Colombia."

"Yes, but he has instant messaging."

Lucy took a deep breath. "Well, that's something. Tell me you have someone else who can bring up the server."

"If you want me to tell you that we have someone else, I will. We have someone else."

He was playing a game she didn't like. "But you don't, do you?"

"No, unfortunately, that person was not in our budget."

"Don't tell me this."

"Okay. I won't tell you this." He got up and put on a gray jacket, obviously getting ready to leave.

"Wait. What I mean is…is there anyone else who can help us?"

"I'm sure there is, but they do not work here."

Lucy sat down in the visitor's chair, trying desperately to keep a positive attitude, but she was having considerable difficulty, given the status of events. "Okay, what do you suggest we do?"

"It's late, Lucia, and I am tired of problems. My wife, she waits. Time to go home." He walked past her.

"But what about the server?" She followed him into the next room.

"Frank will return tomorrow. Maybe he can fix. Maybe not, but until then, may I suggest you enjoy *Italia*. Goodnight, Lucia." And he walked out to the front lobby and, no doubt, out the front door.

"Okay. Fine!" Lucy said out loud, but nobody heard her. The place was entirely empty. The day had been a total disaster. An entire day had been wasted essentially, because she had misjudged everything, but she was simply trying to improve things. Make things happen. Become a mover and a shaker or whatever the hell upper management called themselves.

She walked out to the lobby and sat down in Rosalyn's chair. She was alone in the now-overcrowded lobby while the rest of the company was off somewhere, probably next door, laughing. And she was hungry, almost starving. What she wouldn't give for a simple crust of bread.

Unfortunately, there were many crusts of bread inside the vending machine, but she couldn't bring herself to push any buttons. What if it happened again? What if the lights went out?

She couldn't bear it.

She had tried to get her laptop to work, to do something that would give meaning to her being there, but for some reason, the thing wouldn't cooperate. She couldn't call anyone back home because, well, because she didn't want to.

It was as if life as she knew it had just stopped.

WHEN SHE ENTERED Rosalyn's flat that night, all she cared about was sleep. She turned off her cell phone, deciding she positively didn't want to talk to Dennis or anyone else, for that matter. Sleep was the only cure.

She thought about tying that bell around her toe, if she'd had one, but the way she felt she wouldn't have been able to manage even that. All she really could hope for was that the music wouldn't be too loud, Andrew wouldn't cause her to sneeze too much and Rosalyn wouldn't wake her up in the middle of the night with her Russian lover.

Because tonight, she just wouldn't be able to handle it.

# 13

LUCY STRETCHED and rolled over, totally aware of where she was.

Totally aware of the early-morning light pouring in through the curtainless window.

Aware of the smooth warm sheets surrounding her, and the down pillow cradling her head, the violet color scheme that engulfed the entire room—and the girl staring at her, propped up on one arm, stretched out next to her on the futon. The girl she had never seen before, with violet streaks in her blond hair, a silver hoop protruding from her left eyebrow, and a cigarette burning between her lips.

"I suppose you're her new lover," the girl said with an English accent, staring into Lucy's face.

Lucy reached down under the blankets to her feet and felt for the bell she hoped she had tied to her toe. It wasn't there. She wiggled her feet anyway, just in case she was dreaming and the bell actually was tied to her toe.

Silence.

"You're not Rosalyn," Lucy said, as if it were a fact that the girl didn't know.

"Did you know that she already has a lover?" the girl asked. She wore a ring on every finger and violet nail polish on every nail. She took a long drag on the cigarette and blew the smoke out over Lucy's head.

"Just a minute," Lucy said and held her foot up to get a good look at it. No bell. She asked the girl, "I know this may sound strange, but I have this sleeping problem. Anyway, there are times when I think things are real and they're not, and other times when I think I'm dreaming but I'm not, actually, dreaming... actually. Which are you?"

"Very real," she whispered in a seductive voice, leaning in closer. "Want to touch?"

Lucy moved away. "I'm not in the touching mood," she said and pulled the blankets up around her chin. "Who are you?"

"No. I go first. Who are you?"

The girl sat up: short, wispy hair, a tight purple shirt, and jeans with a rather large belt. Too large, Lucy thought. Not that this was exactly the time or place to rate this girl's accessories, but still... "Lucy Mastronardo. I'm from California. I came here to—"

"Steal my girlfriend?"

"Rosalyn? No, she's not...I'm getting married on Saturday."

"Does she know you're out whoring around with another woman?" The girl got up off the futon and sat in a chair.

Tall. Tall with muscular arms, Lucy thought. She must live at a gym.

Lucy stared as the girl crossed her legs while lounging in the chair. DKNY boots, the same purple boots Lucy had seen at Macy's in Stanford Mall in Palo Alto. They looked better in black.

The girl's question finally sunk in. "No. I mean, I'm not whoring around. I'm marrying a man, not that it matters, but this isn't what it looks like. Where is Rosalyn, anyway?" Lucy gazed around the tiny room, the messy tiny room, now that the Amazon in purple boots had arrived. An electric guitar leaned against the far wall and clothes, shoes, open suitcases and an open guitar case now cluttered every inch of floor space. She'd apparently unpacked by dropping her things wherever she stood.

"You tell me," the girl demanded. "I thought I would surprise her and come back early from my tour, but instead I find *you* in my bed."

"This is *your* bed?" Lucy sat up, so utterly uncomfortable that she'd give anything if this were one of her dreams, a big nightmare of a dream where she could wake up screaming. But this was apparently reality, and lately, reality sucked.

"Yes, and I want you out of it. And you can tell that little slut, Rosalyn, to come and get her shit or I'll throw it out on the street."

Lucy got out of bed, calmly walked to the bathroom, stepped inside and shut the door. Two seconds later, the door opened and Andrew came sliding in. "You can take her damn cat, too. I hate cats."

The girl slammed the door shut.

Lucy sneezed.

FEELING totally desperate and completely humiliated, Lucy decided to swallow her pride and try the Santa Maria again, but the staff just didn't want to cooperate.

"The Santa Maria does not accept pets," the middle-aged, balding front-desk clerk told Lucy for the second time, and for the second time Lucy gave him the same argument. They spoke in Italian.

"Look, he's not my cat. I don't intend to keep him in my room. I'll bring him to his owner as soon as I register. All I want to do is register for a room before they're all gone. I have to sleep in a real bed tonight. Alone."

Andrew sat at her feet on the plush red carpet, looking content on his impromptu leash made from the mouse cord to her laptop. It was the only thing she could think of to use when she and Andrew had been thrown out on the street, homeless.

"Your sleeping habits are not my concern. My concern is a pet, and you cannot bring a pet into the Santa Maria."

Lucy was beyond any semblance of rational behavior as she stood in the lobby of the grand old hotel, begging for a room, a room she deserved, a room she needed. She wanted to haul off and belt the guy right in his puckered kisser. "Perhaps I'm not making myself clear. I do not intend to keep the cat. I'm allergic to cats."

"So is my wife," the man said. "She gets a headache and turns into a miserable, nagging witch. Just one cat hair can cause this nasty change, therefore, please remove your animal at once."

"Listen Mr. Fancy Pants, I have a reservation at this hotel. You will honor that reservation or I'll—"

"You'll do what?"

"I'll call somebody, that's what."

He leaned in, "Whom might you call? Your daddy, perhaps?"

Lucy couldn't believe the arrogance of this really unattractive man. Unfortunately, he had rendered her speechless. She stood huffing and sighing, totally angry and totally unable to come up with a valid argument.

He continued, "You *had* a reservation. It expired on Monday evening when you didn't show up."

"I *had* some difficulty getting here," she told him.

"You *should* have phoned."

"That was impossible."

"Holding your reservation became impossible."

"I demand a room!" She slammed her hand on the desk. Her voice, loud.

He sighed. "The Santa Maria does not accept pets. Kindly step aside."

"I keep telling you, this is not my cat. I'm only holding onto him until I can drop him off with his owner which should be in a couple hours. I just want to change my clothes, put on some makeup and relax before I go to work."

"You cannot bring that creature into a room even for a moment."

The nasty man busied himself with some papers on the desk, further annoying Lucy.

"Then I'll leave him down here tied to a chair."

"Impossible!"

"Why? What harm can a little cat do?"

He paused and looked squarely into her eyes. "Please remove yourself and your furry rat from my lobby or I will be forced to call the police." He then looked beyond her to the young couple in line waiting to check in. "Next," he said in a terse little voice.

The couple didn't move.

Lucy didn't move.

Andrew moved.

He calmly jumped up on the desk and headed straight for Mr. Fancy Pants. With one great swoop, the man was instantly covered in a thick layer of Andrew's hair. Everyone laughed. Mr. Fancy Pants got very red, his eyes bugged out and his neck actually looked as if it was expanding.

Lucy grabbed Andrew and her suitcase and ran out of the hotel, laughing.

"You really are human," she said when they were far enough away so she could stop running. She put him down, pulled her last tissue out of her purse and blew her nose. "Now what?" she asked him, as if he could answer.

He slid his little body across her ankles. She actually liked it. Loved it. An emotion she hadn't expected ever to feel for a cat. Not that she disliked cats, she just had never been around one before. This one made her believe they were genuinely clever. Very clever.

Andrew jumped up on top of Lucy's suitcase, sat himself down by the handle and waited. "You ready to rock and roll?" she asked.

And right on cue, Andrew meowed. She tipped the case on its wheels, Andrew dug in his claws, and off they went as if this were their daily routine.

As she walked down the narrow alley in search of a cab, she decided to review her situation.

Okay, so she had been thrown out of the only place to sleep in town by an angry lesbian who thought she was her old lover's new lover.

Not a problem.

She had handled the totally awkward moment quite well. Seth would never have to know. He'd only make fun of her for allowing herself to be in the situation in the first place. She would simply let it dissolve from her memory. Let it completely fade away, like an old photo caught in the sun.

Okay, so she had blown some massive fuse at Subito and everything had gone down, but Frank was on his way.

Problem solved.

Okay, so she couldn't get a room at the Santa Maria. There were other hotels, just none in the immediate area. She would go back to work and let Rosalyn use her connections.

Problem solved. Over and done with. So far so good.

It started to rain.

Okay, it was raining and she didn't have an umbrella. The least of her worries. After all, how hard could it rain before she found a cab?

The rain intensified. Lucy walked faster. Andrew hunkered down on the suitcase hiding his nose between his front paws.

She held her purse over her head, hoping it would shield her hair, not that her hair looked even remotely good, but she didn't want it wet. Wet, bad hair was the pits. How could anyone take her seriously if she showed up with really yucky hair?

Okay, she was starting to think like a seven-year-old now. That's just great, she thought as she splashed through the puddles, thankful that she had had the foresight to bring a pair of decent boots. At least they kept her feet dry. That had to count for something.

She darted under an awning and made a phone call to Subito. "Come on," she said into the phone. "Answer the damn phone!"

But no one did.

Fine!

She would *not* leave a message.

She slipped the phone into a pocket and looked down the street for a cab, only to realize that for some reason there were no cars on this tiny brick street without sidewalks, only Vespas and motorcycles parked at weird angles next to the ancient row of colorful townhouses that jutted into the road.

A shrine to some saint she didn't recognize adorned a wall about half way down the block. A woman was passing it carrying a little boy on her hip, balancing a covered tray in her other hand. The child held a huge black umbrella over both of them, protesting his job. Lucy wondered if they were having a hooky day. She froze on the thought for a moment, then the rain started to really pound the pavement in great big downpour-type drops.

She hated rain. Especially Italian rain. She so wished she had never agreed to this adventure. That she were home, in her blue cubicle calling Giovanni for his status report.

For a moment she thought about going back to the Santa Maria, but felt certain that if she did, Andrew would end up in some kitty prison and she would be carted off to a dismal Italian jail for irritating a front-desk clerk. Never underestimate an angry Italian with a crazed wife.

She needed a pill or a drink, or something to take away the anxiety, but for now, she'd settle for a dry taxi. She knew she looked bad enough already; no makeup, hair clipped up, a wrinkled blouse, a skirt that was too long and bulky, boots that didn't match the outfit. Not that anyone with any sense of style—which would be the whole of *Napoli*—would call what she was wearing an outfit, but at least her feet were stylish and dry. And at that exact moment, nothing else mattered but her dry, warm feet.

The rain eased up a little so she took a couple steps out from under her awning haven, completely unaware of the motor scooter that came up behind her, nearly knocking her down, but scaring Andrew so badly he ran off. His mouse-leash smashed on the street.

Lucy ran after him, until one of the wheels on her suitcase got stuck in a small hole and stopped her, dead. She pulled and pulled until it finally came free, ripping out the bottom.

"Andrew!" she yelled, as she dragged the now-torn suitcase, her things falling out as she ran. She hesitated, but then continued, hoping for the best. Hoping that not everything would fall out. She spotted the cat darting behind a planter in front of a shop.

"Come on, Andrew. It's all right. Here kitty, kitty, kitty," she called, while thinking how incredibly stupid it was to be chasing after a cat. She didn't even like cats, and this particular cat had gotten her thrown out of the only decent hotel for miles. And oh, how she longed for a room with a comfortable bed and clean white sheets and a huge shower with one of those pulsating heads to massage her back and neck.

She sneezed.

"Come on out, Andrew, you mangy little...here kitty, kitty, kitty."

Another sneeze, only this time a chill ran through her from the rain. She searched her purse for another tissue. She couldn't find one. Perhaps she could buy some tissues inside the shop. She glanced through the window. Everything looked dark for a moment. Then someone moved and she could see clear through.

And there inside the shop, standing next to a girl—a skinny, blond girl—was Vittorio. They were laughing, holding hands, ordering something from a man behind a counter. The shop looked like some sort of gourmet food store, little bins of seeds and beans, baskets of weird mushrooms and fruits, colored oils in tall bottles and strings of red peppers, garlic and herbs hanging from the rafters.

Vittorio looked up toward the window. Lucy ducked down. Her heart raced. Had he seen her? She couldn't be sure, but with his ego, he'd probably think she was following him. All she wanted to do was catch Andrew and get the hell out of there before he came out of the shop.

Unfortunately, Andrew had wedged himself between a flower pot and a wall and Lucy couldn't get at him. "Come on out, Andrew. I'll buy you a whole fish if you come out." Andrew cried and moved in tighter to the wall. Lucy stretched and reached as far as she could, just barely touching his wet fur, mumbling, "Come out of there you ungrateful little—" she said. But as the rain steadily fell, she lost sight of him. Suddenly, somebody pulled her into a narrow walkway around the corner.

"Take off your boots," a man in black said in clear, American English.

"What?"

They were staring at each other.

Face to face.

Eye to eye.

She and some low-down-dirty thief were in a face-off.

This is creepy, she thought.

"Keep your purse and the suitcase. Give me your boots. They're Steve Madden, right?"

"Yes, this season's."

"Size seven and a half?"

"Maddens tend to run a little small, they're an eight, actually, but—"

She didn't understand what was going on. It was the

strangest robbery, if this was a robbery, she had ever heard of.

"Take them off or I'll slug you." He held her by her jacket lapels, close, under his umbrella. She noticed the label on his so-now pea coat, Tommy Hilfiger. His umbrella was Ralph Lauren, and his stocking cap was Gucci.

Gucci made stocking caps?

She looked into his eyes. He didn't look nuts, a little overly label-conscious perhaps, but nothing more than any other young man of say, nineteen, would be. So why did he need to steal her boots?

"Is this a joke? Did my mother send you? Is your name Donico?" she asked.

He pulled her in tighter. "You talk too much. The boots, lady."

"But it's raining. My feet will freeze. Wouldn't you rather take my purse? It's Coach."

He threw her purse on the ground. Everything fell out of it. "I want the boots. Now!"

"All right!" she said and bent over to unzip each boot, not quite believing she was actually being robbed for her footwear.

Wasn't this Italy? The shoe Mecca? Didn't Italians make some of the best shoes in the world? Why would anyone steal Steve Madden boots when they lived in shoe Mecca? She blamed the whole thing on the whim she'd had to buy a trendy pair of boots. This is exactly what trendiness leads to. Thievery.

When Lucy finally pulled off the boots, and that alone was a struggle—it wasn't easy getting out of knee-high wet boots while standing in a rainstorm—she was left in her sheer stockings that immediately tore on the cold, rough pavement.

He shoved her down and ran away, hiding her boots under his pea coat, a stolen pea coat, no doubt. She simply watched as the label-conscious boot thief disappeared into the downpour.

Actually unable to think, she reached over and shoved everything back into her purse, but her precious bottle of tranquilizers along with an eyeliner and a couple of tampons had vanished down a steel grate.

"Fine! Who needs drugs and tampons, anyway," she said out loud.

Lucy stood up, straightened herself out and retraced her steps. When she turned the corner, she stopped. Her clothes lay stuck to the street like dead fish on the shore. Shoes, shirts, pants and underwear littered the now-deserted alley in a long path. She started to pick everything up, but when she found the red Chanel scarf covered in black grease, she sat right down, folded her legs and cried.

Andrew jumped into her lap.

# 14

THERE SHE WAS, sitting in the street like a beggar. Vittorio could hardly believe his eyes. He thought he should walk right by her, saying nothing, but who sits in the street? These Americans, he thought, they are strange people. "Lucia, why you sit here, in the street?" he asked bending down to her level, holding a big black umbrella over the two of them. He had been shopping for fennel seeds when he had seen her standing outside under the awning, then, before he could get to her she was gone.

Now, she sat in the street, in the wet street. He just didn't understand this woman. She made no sense. She was unsensable.

"It's ruined," she told him holding up the scarf, crying. "It will never be the same."

He took the scarf and examined it. "A little soap. A little water. Brand new!"

"No," she said. "It's trash. Simple red trash. Like everything else in my life."

He looked up as a motor scooter whizzed by, that's when he noticed her clothes strewn along the street.

"What happened?" he asked.

"I don't really know," she said wiping her tears on her sleeve. "One minute I was reaching for Andrew, and the next I was being robbed."

Vittorio didn't understand, she was holding her

purse, tight, against her chest. "But you have your purse, no?"

"Uh-huh. He didn't want my purse. It's Coach, you know. I offered, but he didn't want it." She held it up for him to see. "Isn't it a pretty purse? You'd want it, wouldn't you, if you were a thief?"

"Of course," he said, but he was completely perplexed. He looked at her feet, stockings ripped, toes poking out between the holes. "But where are your shoes, Lucia?"

"He's got them."

"Andrew?"

"No, the thief."

He smiled. Now he understood. At least she was not hurt. "Ah, Lucia. I am sorry. We will report this to the police. Come. I will bring you home first." He tried to lift her, but she wouldn't budge.

"That's the problem. I have no home. I'm completely homeless in *Napoli*," she said. "I have a nice apartment back in San Jose. It's a pretty apartment, but that doesn't seem to matter much here. I can't even get a room in a hotel. Not since Andrew."

Vittorio looked around. "But who is this Andrew?"

"He's half human, you know."

"Only half?"

"Yes, and part alley cat."

He couldn't understand what a girl like Lucia would see in a man like that. He sounded terrible, like a bad person. "He's not the man for you."

"Oh, like you would know."

"I know men. Let me take you home, make you a nice frittata. Some good strong coffee. Forget about this Andrew."

"I can't," she said and opened up her jacket to reveal Andrew, who looked up at Vittorio and meowed.

"What is this?"

"This is Andrew," she said.

Vittorio couldn't help but laugh at his own silly jealousy. This woman was, after all, an American who would be out of his life forever in a couple of days, and he had been jealous over a cat. It made him wonder about his feelings for her.

Lucy looked up at him. What a face, he thought. Men would do almost anything for a face like hers. It's magnificent.

"Is the blonde invited, too?" she asked, a touch of sarcasm in her voice. Vittorio didn't like it when she accused without knowing the facts.

"What blonde?" he answered wanting to extend whatever conversation she would have with him, even if it meant he would have to listen to her sharp tongue.

"From the store?"

He paused before answering, watching her eyes, her mouth, thinking of her naked body in his bed. Those full breasts, her stomach, the long legs. He was getting aroused just looking at her.

Finally he said, "Lucia, she is my cousin."

"You know what they say about cousins..."

He didn't get it. "No. What do they say?"

She stared back at him.

He honestly didn't know what she was talking about, and didn't really care. She looked so beautiful sitting there in the rain staring up at him. He wanted to kiss her.

But he didn't.

Instead, she leaned in and kissed him, hard, on the lips. A passionate, warm kiss. A kiss that made Vittorio forget everything he knew about this woman. A kiss that caught him off guard. Made him flush with excitement. Was this real? He couldn't believe his good fortune to have found her. He was glad that he had run out of a simple thing like fennel seeds.

"Take me home, Vittorio," she whispered. "Now," she said and took his hand.

THEY DROVE for a long time, out of the city and down the Amalfi coast. The sea raged as Vittorio cruised along the winding highway. Unexpectedly, Lucy felt completely vulnerable and sorry for herself.

Completely alone.

This was a mistake. A big mistake, she thought.

Lucy wanted to be home, to click her heels together like Dorothy and suddenly be home with her family standing around her bed, holding her hand, stroking her forehead, while she lay under her down blanket. Warm. Safe. The vision was so vivid; her mother bending over her, brown eyes glistening, telling her, "I told you those Neapolitans were thieves. I warned you, but do you ever listen to your mother?" Her father, dressed in Wednesday-wear, "I can set up your laptop right here next to your bed. It'll be just like you're at work." Seth flexing his muscles, giving her a peck on the forehead, whispering, "Does this mean we have to postpone Sexday?"

"No!" she yelled and sat forward in her seat, the seatbelt restraining her from hitting the dashboard.

"Lucia, are you all right? Lucia," a soothing voice echoed in her ears.

She opened her eyes and there he was, sitting next to her, one hand on the stick shift, other hand on the wheel. She must have dozed.

"Vittorio," she said, smiling. He smiled. They were alone, in his car once again, and he was taking her home. There was no place on earth she would rather be at that very moment, than his home. She sat back, her heart still racing with the nightmare, and feeling cold from the rain, but content in knowing she really wasn't in her apartment. She was in Italy, with Vittorio, a man she was falling in love with, or at least falling in lust with. She couldn't be sure. She had never felt these feelings before. Not even with Seth.

Andrew jumped into her lap and made himself comfortable. He was still damp from the rain and looking to get warm. She held him tightly against her, and for once, she didn't sneeze.

Vittorio drove the car over some stones and up a short driveway.

"We are here," he said, smiling, taking her hand in his and kissing it. She watched his lips come down on her hand. Felt the warmth of his mouth.

Delicious, she thought.

The rain had stopped and the sun peeked out from the billowy clouds. The air smelled clean and wonderful as Vittorio held the door open while she stepped out of the car.

She faced a beautiful villa nestled back in the trees.

"I thought we were going to your house?" she said, bewildered.

"This is my house. I buy last year."

"But I thought you lived with your mother?"

"I do. But this is my house."

Vittorio guided her up the stone stairs to the main entrance. Vivid flowers and vines wrapped themselves around each other along the walkway. Drops of rain glistened on the pink and yellow petals. The deep green of the leaves sparkled as she walked up the stairs to the front door, which was surrounded by bright red bougainvillea.

The grounds were amazing, and the house even more amazing. Not that it was very big. Matter of fact, it was rather small, but still incredible. The entire house was made out of stone with beveled-glass windows, and an ornate stained-glass front door.

It looked magical, or at least it looked magical to Lucy, stumbling along in her soaked tan sandals, rescued from the street. They stuck to her feet as she walked. Andrew followed behind them, sniffing everything in his path.

When they got to the top of the stairs, Vittorio opened the front door and stood back, allowing her to walk in first. Ivory walls, arched doorways, traditional Italian tile on the floor and black marble surrounded the large fireplace. There were floor-to-ceiling windows with breathtaking views of the sea, but not one piece of furniture. Not a chair, an ottoman, or even a rug to warm her cold feet. The enchanting villa was entirely empty.

Disappointment rocked her aching body. All she wanted was a chair to fall into, one lousy, stinking chair.

"Stay here much?" she asked.

"Not enough."

"Obviously."

"Do not worry," he said and guided her to the bedroom. "You will be comfortable."

Lucy slipped out of her shoes. She couldn't stand wearing them. The tile felt smooth and cool under her ravaged feet. She was at least thankful for that. Andrew made himself at home in a sunny corner and stretched out with a tiny I'm-home sigh.

Lucy followed Vittorio to the bedroom. Once she stepped inside, her eyes actually welled up as she surveyed what had to be the most enticing bedroom she had ever seen.

"You will be comfortable here. You may consider this yours for as long as you would like," he said as he walked to the far wall to open the French doors.

"It's beautiful," she said. There was a queen-size bed dressed in a deep-wine-colored comforter and filled with an assortment of euro-sized pillows that Lucy couldn't wait to fall into. Sheer white curtains hung from the ceiling, surrounding the vintage walnut bed. The walls were sponged in shades of tan, white and a dark gold, giving the room a warm, inviting ambiance.

Three colorful area rugs adorned the floor: one next to the bed, one leading to the doors, and one in front of a brown chaise in the left corner of the room. There were a couple of walnut dressers, and a nightstand. A child's rocking chair sat in the corner.

"Yours?" she asked, pointing to the small rocker.

"Yes. My father, he made for me when I was small. I have to keep. Someday, I will give it to my son...or daughter." He smiled. She liked it when he smiled. "You can wash in here," he said and opened a door.

The bathroom was entirely covered in green marble with a sunken tub. Clear glass doors surrounded a separate fabulous shower stall. How Lucy yearned for a long, hot shower.

"I bring in your things. You rest and when you wake, we eat. Okay?"

"Okay," she said and watched him as he left the

room. At least for now, the room was all hers, and for now, it was all she needed.

For a moment, Lucy didn't know what to do first. A tinge of guilt raced through her, guilt about the project and Subito. She should call Dennis. Call marketing. Call somebody and tell them…tell them what? That the systems were down because she'd installed a couple of vending machines? That the chip would probably not go out on time? That they could fire her sorry ass whenever they wanted to because she was, after all, worthless? She could feel herself heading for the pity-potty when she suddenly flashed on Seth. Her fiancé. The perfect man for her. The man she was marrying on Saturday.

This Saturday.

Or was she?

As she stood under the hot water in Vittorio's oh-so-fabulous shower, she thought about Seth and marriage, Saturday and mai tai fountains, and for some totally random reason, her indecisiveness flew out the open French doors and she knew what she had to do.

# 15

"HELLO," her mother said, but Lucy could hear the tension in her voice.

"Hi, Mom. It's me."

"Finally, you call, it's the middle of the night, but it's all right. My feet are burning me up. Where are you?"

"I'm still in Italy, Mom."

"But, you're not alone."

Lucy wondered how her mother knew these things.

"No."

"I thought so. Now what?"

Lucy could hear her father in the background wanting to know who was on the phone. Her mother told him to go back to sleep, that everything was fine. It was only Lucy. "Tell her I love her and not to worry. Everything's all set for Saturday," he said. Then Lucy heard him punch his pillow and settle down.

Her mother whispered into the phone. "Go ahead, Lucia. Your father went back to sleep."

"I have to postpone the wedding," Lucy said. The words caught in her throat.

"I already gave the relatives a warning."

"What do you mean? Why would you tell anyone—"

"They gotta know, don't they? No daughter of mine goes off to Italy a week before her wedding without her mother knowing what she's doing. I know you don't want to marry Seth."

"So, now you know his name? Before you could never think of it, and now that I want to postpone the wedding you can remember it."

"Now, it's important. Before, it didn't matter."

"You make me crazy, you know that?"

"I'm supposed to. I'm your mother. Do you love him?"

"Who?"

"The guy you're not alone with?"

"I don't know what I feel for him. All I know is he makes me laugh." She let out a tearful sigh. "Oh, Mom. I'm so confused. All my life I've known exactly what I wanted, and what I had to do to get it, and suddenly I'm not so sure anymore."

"You think you have some control over your life? Over who you love and who you don't love? I don't think so. You can't force your heart to do what is logical. A heart is not one of them computers you work on all day. A heart does what it wants to do, while your head tells you what you have to do."

Lucy began to cry. She longed for her mother's embrace. To be held and cuddled and told it would all work out for the best. "Oh Mamma, I don't know what to do."

"Then don't do anything. Sometimes in life you have to stop and let things happen."

"But I can't get married on Saturday. I just can't."

"Call him. You can do that much. Then you can collapse and have a good cry. You'll feel better."

"But what about the caterer and the florist and the limo—"

"What? You think me and your father can't take care of these things?

"But the expense of it all."

"So who says we have to lose anything? You think your mother is dumb? I'm not so dumb. I got a few ideas of my own."

"Thank you, Mom."

"I love you too, my heart."

They spoke a little more about the wedding, Seth, and what Lucy would do next. When they hung up, Lucy actually felt better.

Until she tried to call Seth. He didn't answer.

Odd, she thought. But perhaps he was just sound asleep or he'd gone into work really early, or he's asleep under his desk. She left a message for him to give her a call when he got up. She took a deep breath and dialed his work number, just in case. When the message came on she hung up and tried his cell. He didn't answer. She left another message for him to call her, but thought it strange that she couldn't get him on any of his numbers.

Suddenly she was very sleepy, but this time she would tie that bell to her toe as she had promised her mother. Vittorio's rocking chair had several tiny bells stitched along the top. She borrowed one and tied it to her big toe, just in case.

She turned off her phone, thinking that when Seth did call, she needed to be wide awake, and this time, Lucy, feeling somewhat content for the first time since she had arrived, drifted off to blissful sleep in Vittorio's queen-size bed.

WHEN SHE AWOKE in that amazing room, alone, the first thing she did was ring her bell.

Ring. Ring.

Nothing changed.

Ring. Ring.

Again, nothing changed.

She looked around. It's true, she thought. I'm really here. Alone in my very own bed in Vittorio's house in Italy. A great big smile and a feeling of total happiness washed over her as she stretched. She slid out of bed feeling absolutely fabulous for the first time in, well, like forever.

The view from the open French doors that led out to a small but private patio was also amazing. Too amazing, with the azure sea endlessly stretching out in front of her, and the flat red rooftops of the quaint village below, and the surrounding hills covered with lush vegetation jutting out into the water. How could it not be amazing? Everything around her was phenomenal, even the air. She took in a cleansing breath and let it out. Slowly.

She felt completely relaxed and completely starved.

Lucy found a pair of fuzzy slippers, Vittorio's no doubt, and put them on. They felt warm and silky despite the fact that they were about thirty sizes too big.

She made her way through the house guided by the smell of something cooking, bread or cookies perhaps. It made her walk even faster until she came to the kitchen, where Vittorio stood with his back to her, pulling a dish out of a packed refrigerator.

Ah, the kitchen. And what did she expect? He was a chef, after all.

The kitchen was right out of "Better Homes," or was there some culinary magazine that showcased cool kitchens? And if there was, Lucy thought, this kitchen would definitely make the cover—totally modern and totally stocked with every pot, pan and kitchen gizmo Emeril could ever need. Besides all the gadgets and steel appliances, there was a huge black marble counter that sat at least eight people. There was even a small pizza oven, just like her mother had.

Every burner on the double-wide gas stove had a pot frying or boiling something. Every inch of counter space had a bowl or a plate waiting to be filled. The mixer was mixing and the blender was blending. Whatever meal Vittorio had planned for her was enough to feed his whole restaurant.

Lucy sat down on one of the black leather-and-chrome bar stools along the counter, yawned, and waited for Vittorio to turn around, while she wiggled her now itching toes.

EVERYTHING had to be perfect. He couldn't take any chances. He felt as if it were a test, a trial kind of a thing. If he didn't handle her with the utmost care, he would ruin his chance forever.

He had planned a small meal. Something easy, but the easy had gone too fast and he had decided to add a few side dishes. The side dishes turned into many little meals and the many little meals demanded desserts, and well, before he knew it, he had prepared enough food for three days. He figured perhaps she would stay that long, if for no other reason than to dine on his tempting culinary treats.

He heard her yawn behind him. He turned, holding a raspberry white chocolate torte. It was the dessert he was famous for in *Napoli*, and he wanted her to try it.

"Lucia, you are awake," he said, happy to see her sitting across from him, wearing his pajamas. The light from the window behind her illuminated the thin material and he could see the outline of her breasts.

"*Magnifico!*" he exclaimed.

"Is that for me, or for whatever that luscious-looking thing is in your hand?" she asked, leaning forward to get a better look. Her hair was piled up high on her head, and she had that just-woke-up look that Vittorio loved in a woman. He wanted to go around the counter and hold her, tight, next to his body, but they hadn't gotten that far yet.

Perhaps later.

A man could only hope.

"*Magnifico* is for you. Only God can make such a perfect woman. I am but a man. I can only make the perfect torte," he said, feigning coy. She laughed.

This was a good beginning, he thought.

LUCY HAD DECIDED just to let it be, his charm, that is. Actually, it was refreshing to be so worshiped, so doted on, so taken care of, and the one thing she really needed right now was a lot of doting. And who better to dote on a woman, than a gorgeous man who cooked. Was there any more perfect dream?

"What is that?" she asked while pointing to the red-and-white delicacy in his hand.

"This will delight you almost as much as I can."

She smiled again. "I'm in need of delight. Can I try it right now?"

"Me or the torte?" he asked, grinning that sly grin of his. It made his eyes sparkle, and she was a sucker for sparkling eyes.

"The torte," she said, catching his grin.

Vittorio carefully removed the torte from the baking dish, put it on a creamy-green platter, sliced off a piece, slid it onto a white dessert plate, surrounded it with a raspberry sauce, sprinkled it with white chocolate slivers and eased the plate in front of Lucy.

Before she could take a bite, her mouth was watering with anticipation.

She cut into it: raspberries, custard and white chocolate oozed onto her fork. Vittorio waited as she took a bite.

"Oh my God!" she mumbled. "Way too good." She took another bite. "It's so smooth. I love white chocolate, but this is...heaven."

He took the plate away from her. She tried to grab it. He said, "We will have after dinner. First a little salad, a little soup, a bite of pasta, a little wine, this and that, and we come back to the torte."

Lucy tried to snitch another bite. Had her fork in mid-air, but Vittorio was adamant.

"Look at all this," she chided, sweeping her arm across the counter. "Feed me. I can't wait anymore."

It was almost as if he were taunting her with food. What a concept, she thought. To be teased with the smells and visuals of incredibly irresistible culinary pleasures. She just couldn't stand the temptation another moment.

Her mouth watered.

Her stomach growled.

"Come. We eat, yes?" he said and walked out through a back door off the kitchen.

"Yes," she answered, following him into a large glass-enclosed room with another breathtaking view of the sea. A small table was set for two with white linen, silver and crystal. The rain threatened to return, but she felt warm and cozy standing next to the heat from the fireplace. She felt absolutely sure she was in some kind of old movie and somebody was going to yell "Cut!" before she could actually sit down and enjoy the moment.

"Am I really here?" she said to herself, but Vittorio overheard her.

"Yes," he answered and kissed her gently on the lips. They stopped for a moment, staring at each other. He held her in his arms, close, encircling her with his body. She wanted to kiss him again, harder this time, with all the power of the love she felt for him, but she knew she couldn't. Knew that if she did, she wouldn't stop and it would be wrong. Wrong because she hadn't spoken to Seth. Hadn't told him that she didn't love him anymore, probably never had. Not really. Not the way you were supposed to love the man you were marrying. She couldn't marry Seth on Saturday.

Not this Saturday.

Not ever.

"I can't," she said, pulling herself away from his embrace. "It's not right. This whole thing isn't right."

"You are worried about your wedding?"

"Yes. I'm worried about my fiancé. I need to talk to him and I can't get him on the phone. I'm worried that I might be making a big mistake. That this—"

He stopped her from rambling on. "Then we will wait until you talk to him. You will know what is the right thing to do after you hear his voice."

"Yes. I think I will," she said, wanting his arms around her again. Wanting to feel his lips on hers again.

"Well, I think it is time for supper. Yes?"

"Supper. Yes," she said vocalizing the tension away.

He put his arm around her shoulder and seated her at the table.

"You sit. Enjoy. I bring the food," he said and disappeared into the kitchen.

# 16

SUPPER was more than she had expected, more delicious, more sensual, and much more filling. With each dish, Vittorio would describe in detail what she was eating and how he had blended the flavors in such a way that no one else in all of *Italia* could come up with his secret combinations.

She agreed and just kept eating.

"For the appetizer I have prepared Tuna-Artichoke Carpaccio, an appetizer featuring spicy marinated raw tuna over a succulent bed of lemon-marinated artichoke hearts."

Suddenly his English had improved, and he sounded like an ad in *Italian Cooking* magazine. He made her laugh, and she hadn't laughed, really laughed, in a very long time.

He had gone on like that throughout the entire feast, and when it came time for dessert, Lucy decided to stop herself. She didn't want to end up as she had at the Santa Maria. It would be even more embarrassing this time.

"Umm, that was marvelous," she said. "Where did you learn to cook like that?"

"When I was a boy I would watch my mother, then my uncle Roberto taught me in his restaurant, La Bella Note. He was the best."

"La Bella Note belonged to your uncle?"

"Yes," he said. "Let us go out to the patio with our wine. The view is good."

Vittorio grabbed a couple of blankets from the bedroom, Lucy grabbed the wineglasses and the bottle and they made their way outside to the patio.

The sky was awash with pinks and grays. Clouds sat in layers, caressed by color. Dusk was upon them and it was spectacular. It reminded Lucy of what she had been missing, and for one night, it was good to be able to enjoy her parents' homeland.

They sat on a double-wide chaise lounge, propped their feet up, and cuddled together. The air was cold and damp, but it was warm and comfortable under the blankets.

"So tell me more about your uncle's restaurant and how you learned to cook."

"Ah, it is a boring story. Let's talk about you."

"Maybe later. I would really like to hear how you learned to cook so well. I can barely fry an egg."

He leaned in closer and gently kissed her on the cheek. She responded with warmth and affection, perhaps too much affection. She could really get to like this.

"My uncle, Roberto, was a good man. My mother's brother. He loved to cook and I loved to watch him. It was the way he did it, with passion. Like he was making love to the food. He had to smell every piece of fruit, taste every vegetable, every seed, or herb. He grew his own herbs."

"Do you?"

"I wish I could, but no. I no have the time. The restaurant is too busy. I need to buy...at the shop where we meet this morning."

She nodded her recognition.

He continued, "Perhaps when I open my restaurant in San Francisco I will grow my own herbs. That is why we meet on the plane. I come back from San Francisco."

"Why would you want to leave all this?"

"So the people in San Francisco can eat my wonderful food."

She laughed. "No. Really."

"My mamma, she deserve the best. I want to give the best to her. She can run this restaurant, and I run the other. That way, we are both happy. Now, sometimes, too many cooks. You know?"

"Yes, I know what you mean. So what was the first thing you ever made?"

"A flan. Miserable, this flan. I forget the sugar. And I served it to my uncle who spit it out and slapped me for it in front of everybody."

"That's awful!"

"For you, maybe. For me? I never forget the sugar again. He taught me to taste everything before I serve. If I don't like, the people no like. Makes sense, no?"

"Yes, but it's a hard way to learn."

Vittorio smiled and shook his head.

"That's the best kind. You never forget."

"Did you like your uncle?"

"I love my uncle. He was better to me than my own father. When my uncle die, he leave me the restaurant. When my father die, he only leave me alone. My father, he wasn't a good man."

"I'm sorry."

"He liked women too much."

"Like you?"

He blushed. "But, I am not married."

Lucy hesitated, but wanted to know how he felt about marriage.

"Do you want to be?" she asked.

"Maybe yes, maybe no. The answer is part of my future."

"Sounds like you're not sure."

"I am not like you. I cannot always know what to do."

"Lately, I'm not sure about anything," she said, taking his hand.

"Then, for now, this is enough."

"Yes, for now."

They kissed again, then he pulled away.

"Now, it is your turn to tell me about what you like."

That's a first, Lucy thought. No guy, including Seth, had ever asked her, with any genuine interest, what she really wanted out of life. However, she was still somewhat skeptical that he would actually listen.

"Let's see. I want to be the director of program managers at B-Logic."

"That's nice, but what do you want from this life."

Lucy thought for a moment. Her work was her life. What did he mean? "But that's what I want."

"No. That is a job. You work for somebody else. What do you want for *your* life? What makes you happy? What gives you, how you say, *gen e' se qua?*"

He was asking her the type of questions you talked about while smoking pot in a dark room with incense burning in a Buddha dish. Not that she ever smoked pot, well maybe once or twice in high school, but that was a long time ago. She never really thought about *gen e' se qua* or fulfillment. Not really. She only thought about the next raise, the next promotion, not about what made her soul happy. That was a topic for other people, older people, but not for her. Not yet, anyway.

"I guess I never thought about anything else but electronics. My dad is an electrical engineer. I'm a second-generation. It's all I ever wanted."

"Then, this is your pappa's life. Not yours."

She was getting angry, and she didn't want to get angry. It was such a lovely night.

"Let's talk about you some more."

"Ah, Lucia, this is something we all must decide or we can not breathe."

"I breathe just fine, thank you."

She felt the tension mounting. Felt the agitation building. She didn't want to talk about the needs of her soul. Didn't want to think about it. Not now. Not with Vittorio.

She looked away.

It was dark now. The color had vanished from the sky. Nothing below her but the lights from the other villas along the water. It wasn't as pretty. Wasn't as glamorous. She wanted to run away, or at least get up and go in the other room, but Vittorio kept her hand in his.

"We talk about some other time," he said and kissed her ever so gently. Almost a brush of a kiss.

It took everything that was in her not to succumb to the moment. It would have been so easy to make love to Vittorio right there on the patio, under the stars, with the lights twinkling below, only she was engaged to another man.

A man she now realized she had truly never loved.

"So tell me more about your dream restaurant in San Francisco," she whispered.

He leaned back on the chair, "Ah, San Francisco—"

# 17

WHEN LUCY awoke on Thursday morning, she felt completely miserable. Her head ached from years of Catholic guilt.

What had she done?

She was in bed, albeit alone, but it was still *his* bed. Vittorio's bed. A guy she had just met. A guy she knew nothing about, other than that he was an Italian chef.

Okay, so maybe she knew a little more about him than just the chef part. They *had* talked for hours the previous night before sleep claimed them.

So, other than the incredible food and titillation stuff, what the hell was she doing with him? And what about Seth? Remember him? The trusting, honorable Boy-Scout fiancé? She reached for her phone and turned it on.

Nothing. It was completely dead.

Okay, that was even worse. Even if Seth had wanted to return her call, he couldn't. Perhaps, by now, her mother had called him and told him about the postponed wedding and he had done something drastic. Something terrible. Something horrible!

She buried her head in the pillow.

The down pillow smelled of lilacs, or was it roses? She couldn't tell. She never did know the distinct scents of flowers. She took in another breath, burying her nose even deeper in its fragrance. It was definitely something sweet.

What if it was another woman's perfume? The thought made her sit up straight. Made her jealous. There she was feeling jealousy over another woman when she herself was cheating on her own fiancé. Wasn't it a sin that she even *thought* about having sex with Vittorio—wonderful, passionate sex that would linger in her memory for days and give her a shiver just to think of it?

This was most definitely sinful.

She decided she was going straight to hell. If she died in that instant from some kind of brain explosion there would be no pearly gates for her. Oh no. Not for this mind-cheating babe. Just fire and smoke.

She was probably on her way already. Her soul, in all likelihood, was now completely covered with mortal-sin stains, a mark for every time she thought of Vittorio in bed, thought of lying next to him or kissing him, or of having a dozen or so orgasms with him. She tried to count up all the times she had thought just about his kiss, but her head hurt too much to concentrate. As far as she could see, her soul had to be one indistinguishable smudge.

She dropped back down on the bed and covered her head with the blanket and imagined all those old guys who had died while making love to young bimbos. Maybe there was a special place in hell for the sex sinner. A special room or cave, where everyone goes for eternity....

*It's dark. Tormented screams echo all around her. The place reeks of smoke. She coughs. She's trapped in a dark, black cave with unbelievably old, naked, wrinkled men trying to get at her. Smiling. Leering. Their hell is to be con-*

*stantly in the state of orgasm. Twitching. Groaning. Moaning. Shaking.*

The bed moved and something touched her foot. Lucy yanked her foot in tight and screamed.

"Lucia. It's me. You are dreaming."

She uncovered her head and looked at Vittorio sitting next to her on the bed. At first glance he looked as if he had two tiny horns growing out of the top of his head, but after rubbing her eyes, she realized it was his slept-on hair.

He was holding a tiny cup and saucer. "Look," he said. "I bring you espresso."

She sat up, seized the cup and took a sip.

Bitter, but good.

"Thank you," she said. "What time is it? Where's the clock?"

"Why you want a clock in the bedroom? You gonna keep the time on something? What happens in here should not be timed like a baked chicken. Clocks are for kitchens and contests, but not for bedrooms."

She smiled at the romantic logic of it.

He continued. "Do not worry about the time. It is morning. Is that not good?"

She looked into his eyes. He had terrific eyes, Hugh Grant eyes, sincere yet mischievous at the same time. What girl could trust a man with Hugh Grant eyes?

She wanted to tell him, "No. I have to go into work. I have too much to do. Everyone is depending on me." Instead she didn't argue, didn't put up a fuss, pushed Dennis and Giovanni, test, marketing, the future of B-Logic, the chip from hell and her miserable attempt at postponing her wedding right out of her mind. She really and truly wanted only one thing.

"Let's play hooky," she said, jumping out of bed,

twirling around so that the white sheet she was holding wrapped around her as though she were a mummy.

Vittorio watched as she danced around the room like a kid who had just found out she was spending the day at the beach instead of going to school. She jumped and danced and twirled until she fell back on the bed, exhausted. A feeling of complete exhilaration splashed over her as Vittorio held her in his arms.

"I like this game, hooky," he said. "It makes you happy."

"Ecstatic!" she said, pleasantly out of breath.

"You should play more often," he said.

"Yes, I should play much more often," she answered. "What's for breakfast?"

"Espresso," he said.

"I need food, not coffee."

"Get dressed. I drive to Positano. We will have lunch by the sea."

The mere mention of the town reminded Lucy of her mother, and the one person she didn't want to bring into this hooky day was her mother.

"Isn't there somewhere else? My mother says it's a crowded city with too many steps."

"It is perfection this time of year. No tourists. You can shop for new clothes and perhaps see where your mamma, she grow up."

"The shopping part is good, but I'm not too sure about the house-hunting part," she said, hesitating at his offer.

"Lucia, it is time to see."

Actually, she really didn't know why she didn't want to go.

"Maybe for an hour or so," she told him. "But I don't have anything to wear."

"You wear my clothes for now. There are many shops in Positano. You will find something beautiful. I am sure."

"I'm sure," she repeated, smiling.

Vittorio left the room. Lucy stretched, and, with a great deal of apprehension, found her phone charger, plugged it into an outlet, attached her phone and waited for it to instantly ring.

But it didn't.

She waited some more.

Nothing.

She decided to take this phone-silence as a good sign and went over for a quick peek out at the world.

The awesome view was still there. She took in a deep breath as she stood in front of the open French doors. How wonderful to be able to breathe, she thought. To really breathe.

What a concept!

Andrew came wandering in for a morning pet. He was dry and completely content as he slipped around her ankles.

"Hey you. It's nice here, isn't it?" she said while kneeling down to give him a hug. His fur felt warm to her touch. She liked it. Soft. Smooth.

Then she sneezed.

She stood up. "Okay, so I'm still allergic to you. But it's all right. I still like you."

She sneezed again.

Andrew walked back out on the patio. Lucy walked into the bathroom.

After taking a shower and finally putting on some makeup from what she could pick out of the broken and spilled mess at the bottom of her purse, she realized she really and truly had nothing to wear of her own. Every piece of clothing was sopping wet or ruined, even the white Ann Taylor couldn't be salvaged. She threw what she could in Vittorio's washer: black pants, Old Navy pajamas, a cream blouse, a camisole. She threw out what was unsalvageable: all thongs, stockings, a T-shirt, two blouses, and laid out the rest to dry—one white bra, 32C.

The Chanel scarf went into the sink to soak with some very hopeful thoughts.

She slipped on her only pair of dry undies and headed for Vittorio's closet. A swank patterned brown shirt, Versace, hung in a small closet along with a row of equally chic shirts, jackets and slacks. She settled on the Versace and a pair of black Armani drawstring sweat pants that fit if she rolled up the bottoms.

She let her hair fall free and cleaned out her Coach handbag, grabbed her phone and in just under an hour she was ready to visit a place she had been hearing about all her life.

## 18

"IT'S JUST as I imagined it to be," Lucy said as she and Vittorio made their way down endless whitewashed steps on *Via Cristoforo Colombio* in Positano. They were snacking on sweet cakes and sharing a large cappuccino. "I need shoes," she said, and they entered a shop called Costanzo Avitabile where a man and his strange sewing machine crafted her a pair of the most comfortable sandals she'd ever slipped onto her now-tired feet. Her BCBGs just weren't making it. Vittorio bought a pair as well, brown, with cross-stitching on the top.

"I promise, I will not eat these," he told the shoemaker behind the counter when he was paying for the sandals. The short Italian man with the thin, graying hair looked at him. "You eat your shoes?" the man said, earnestly.

"Only when the eggs are bad," Lucy said.

"Then, may I suggest that you soak these in wine first. The leather will be more tender," the shoemaker said, totally straight-faced.

There was that awkward moment of silence, then the three of them laughed out loud. The man shook his head, gave Vittorio his change and said, *"Buona fortuna!"* as the couple left the store.

When they passed Maria Lampo's swimsuit shop, Vittorio made her back up on the stairs. "You cannot leave *Italia* without a famous Italian bikini," he said and pulled her into the store.

Maria Lampo's had to be one of the oldest swimsuit shops in town. "This is where the bikini, she start," Vittorio said as he fingered some of the many colorful suits that encircled them.

"Really? The bikini started here?" Lucy asked.

"I don't know for sure, but, maybe."

"Well, then—" she answered and picked suit after suit off the racks that surrounded them in the over-crowded store. She and Vittorio picked out as many suits as they could hold and a young sales girl directed them to a fitting room. Vittorio tried to join her, but Lucy threw him out.

She modeled several bikinis for him and with each one he kept making her turn around one more time. "Ah, this is good, but go around again." She followed his direction. "Good. Good, but go around again." He made her laugh and forget about everything else in her life but trying on bathing suits.

Finally, she settled on a multicolored one-piece, a two-piece in bright yellow and another two-piece she could only wear in her bathtub. She bought a pair of expensive Blumarine sunglasses, a large straw bag to carry everything in, and threw in a red-hot itsy-bitsy number for Rosalyn, the girl who somehow was responsible for all of this.

They stopped at a lace shop to buy an incredible tablecloth for her mother and at a cheesy souvenir shop just for fun. They stopped at a clothes boutique where Lucy bought an indecently short blue skirt and a white see-through blouse. She wore her bikini top under it. Her hair caressed her shoulders and when she caught a glimpse of herself in a bakery window, she almost didn't recognize that way-too-sexy-looking girl staring back at her.

Just past the bakery she recognized a street name. "I think my mother lived right down here," she told Vittorio, pointing the way. It was a lovely alleyway, lined with bougainvillea, planters overflowing with colorful blooms and shops with their wares out on display.

Vittorio followed behind her as she took a turn down a tight alley to a building with a rose facade. All the buildings in this ancient cliff city were painted in pastels: rose, peach, violet and ivory, with red-tile roofs. And every house had a slant to it, just as every step was worn in the direction of the slope it was built on. There were no real streets in this city, only endless steps. If you owned a car it had to be parked in one of the public parking lots above or below the village. It was the only town built on the vertical, rather than the horizontal. It must be like living in a city filled with San Francisco's Lombard Street. You either liked the physicalness of it or you moved on down the coast to something a little more flat.

Lucy's mother had loved the tug of it, the way it made her thighs burn just to walk to the local bakery.

"This is where she grew up. Right on this street somewhere," Lucy said.

"And it is a lovely street. Come, I know a place where we can eat," he told her. Lucy followed.

The small bistro was hidden inside what looked like a private villa. They climbed the tight staircase to the second floor and walked out on the open terrace where a slight woman sat playing an accordion that was bigger than she was. There was a man sitting next to her playing a mandolin, and between the two of them, the small terrace echoed with traditional music.

Lucy beamed when Vittorio took her hand and twirled her around to the music as they danced their way over to a small table for two overlooking the sea.

"Keep this up, and I'll never go back home," Lucy said when they were seated across from each other.

Vittorio held her hand and said, "Then let us dance all day." He stood up to get her to continue dancing, but Lucy made him sit down. People were staring.

What had she just said? Why had she said it? She blamed her starry-eyed outburst on the moment. On the town. On the turquoise sea below. The place was entirely too romantic, with its huge terra-cotta pots filled with flowers, and the ornate tile, the clear blue sky overhead and intimate tables for two.

And that music. What was up with that? How was a girl supposed to behave normally with that Sorrento song playing in the background?

Lucy tried to regain some composure, like that was remotely possible with Vittorio sitting across from her. Smiling. Looking all sexy-sweet with those boy-like eyes and that sly little grin that actually gave him a slight dimple when the light hit his cheek the way it did at that exact moment.

A red-haired waitress around Lucy's age came over, and Vittorio ordered two sandwiches, a bottle of water and two glasses of "the best" homemade Limoncello. Before the waitress could write everything down, a little boy came running up to her holding a truck in one hand and a Hot Wheels sports car in the other. He had bright red hair and a smile to die for. He spoke Italian. "Maria wants my car. I told her it was mine, but she wants it anyway," he said, almost in tears.

"You know what I said about sharing," the waitress answered playing with his hair.

"Is he yours?" Lucy asked.

"Yes." His mother bent to his level. "Say hello to these nice people. Be a gentleman."

He smiled up at Lucy and her heart melted. He was beautiful. "Hello," he said, smiling, hanging on to his mother.

"Hello. What's your name?" Lucy asked.

"Gataldo," he whispered.

"He's beautiful," Lucy told her, reaching out to caress his silky hair.

"He's a handful," the waitress announced. "When he was born it was like a national holiday. Go play with your cousin," she told him. "I'm working." He ran off to the back of the terrace where a little girl waited for him, sitting on the floor in the shade of a gigantic flower pot. "He's one of three children who were born in this town in the last eight years. He's treated like royalty. You would think he is a king the way some of the older people carry on."

"You are a queen," Vittorio said. "Most Italian women do not want babies. Too interested in their jobs."

"Ah, what kind of life is it to stay home all day and cook and clean and watch kids grow? What do men know of these things?" the waitress said with an edge to her voice.

"We know that you will save our country."

The waitress blushed. "Maybe. But it is not very glamorous, this country-saving thing."

"You are a Madonna," Vittorio said and kissed her hand. The waitress smiled, obviously charmed.

When she left, Lucy's attention was drawn to the view below. The view she had heard of, dreamt of, imagined since she was a toddler in her mother's arms:

the taupe-colored sand of the beach, the brightly colored rowboats, the fisherman mending their nets or sanding their overturned boats, the rows of umbrellas dotting the shoreline, and the peacefulness of the endless turquoise sea. She had envisioned the view a thousand times in her mind, and now to see it made her eyes glisten and her throat tighten.

When she turned back to Vittorio, her brain cloudy with emotion, she wanted to tell him everything. Wanted to tell him exactly what she was feeling. "Vittorio, I—"

That's when her phone rang.

She toyed with not answering. Just ignoring the phone call. She didn't want to talk to anyone. Didn't want to lose the moment, but it was B-Logic's number that flashed across the tiny screen. She had to answer. She turned away from the table.

"Hello," she said into the phone.

"Lucy. Finally. What happened to your phone?" Dennis demanded.

She had to think fast. "I've been having some trouble—"

"Whatever. I've got you now, that's all that matters."

She was sorry she had answered.

He continued. "Giovanni tells me there were some electricity problems over there, but that everything's all right now. However, the link between the sites is down for some reason, something to do with your firewall. You're working to get it resolved, right?"

"Of course," she said with conviction.

"Good, 'cause we can't seem to see any problems here. It has to be on your side. I want to make sure you're on top of it. Are you?"

"Sure thing, Dennis. Right on top."

"Great. I'm going back to bed for a few hours. Give me a call around nine o'clock my time and let me know how things are progressing."

"You got it."

"Good. Oh and just thought you should know, the paperwork for your promotion is sitting on my desk waiting for my signature. Everything's on schedule, right?"

Lucy's chest tightened. That old feeling crept up her spine and into her lungs. That familiar feeling of panic was about to overtake her as she sat on the beautiful terrace, a world away from Silicon Valley. The benefits of modern technology—you could have a panic attack no matter where you were.

She searched her handbag for a pill. She needed a pill. Was desperate for a pill. Then she remembered. They were gone.

She told herself over and over to calm down, but she could feel the panic rising, until Vittorio touched her hand.

"I'll call you with the status," she told Dennis and snapped her phone shut. She wanted to spend the rest of the afternoon sitting right there, across from Vittorio, looking out over the sea, but she couldn't. Not if she wanted to keep her job, and her job was important.

Wasn't it?

"I'm sorry, but I have to go," she said.

"But we just got here," Vittorio answered with genuine sadness in his voice.

"I know, but it's business. That was my boss. I have to go back to *Napoli*."

"Right now?" Vittorio asked.

"Yes," Lucy said and stood up to leave. Vittorio put some money down on the table and they left.

# 19

AFTER A rather quiet drive back to Vittorio's villa, Lucy gathered what was left of her meager possessions and shoved them into her new straw bag. The only thing that had really come through it all was the heavy plastic makeup case from Target. The red Chanel was just too wet to bring along, so she left it behind, along with the Ann Taylor white silk suit and the now-ruined Coach handbag. She picked up a sleepy Andrew and silently got back into Vittorio's Alfa Romeo for what had to be the last time.

Driving back to *Napoli* with the top down, on what's considered to be some of the most hazardous roadway in Italy, Statale 163, where it sometimes reaches four hundred feet above sea level with two skinny lanes that hover over sheer drop-offs on either side, Lucy had a bright idea. "I want to learn how to drive a stick. Would you teach me?"

"Now?" Vittorio asked.

"Why not?"

"But it will take time to learn. I thought you were in a rush to get you back to Subito."

"I am, but when did that ever make a difference to you?"

"But this road is not so good for learning to drive."

"I know how to drive, just not a stick shift. How hard can it be?"

"On this road?"

"It's a good road." He took a corner and a bus nearly sideswiped them. He swore out the window as she held onto the dash. "Okay, so it's a little tight, but I'm a good driver. Look, if I can drive in San Francisco, I can drive anywhere."

"If this is how you want to die, then we die together," he said, grinning.

"All right!" she answered.

He pulled the car over, parked it and they both got out, sharing a gentle kiss, "for good luck," Vittorio whispered, as they passed each other to change seats.

When they got back in, real excitement rushed over Lucy. Finally, she was in the driver's seat, and it felt so wonderfully good. Empowering, even.

He handed her the key. "Put the key in and step on the gas."

"I think I've got that part," she said as the car roared its start.

"Okay, not that much," Vittorio warned, obviously nervous about the whole thing. "Remember, first gear is straight. Okay?"

She watched his hand on the stick, how he gripped it with his palm, how his fingers wrapped around the leather ball, how magnificent his hands were, how smooth, those long perfect fingers.

"Wow!" she said, completely overcome by the moment. Another stain on her over-smudged soul, she was sure.

Vittorio, obviously confused over her rapture, said. "I know, it is really the best thing learning how to drive this car. When I first learned, I, too, was amazed."

Lucy laughed out loud at his momentary innocence, then she leaned over and kissed him on the cheek.

When she pulled away he said, "We can go back to my house if you want."

"No," she said. "I want to learn this."

"Okay, one more time, first gear is straight, okay?"

"Okay." She regained her composure and sat back. "First gear is straight."

"And second gear is back, like this." He pretended to slide the stick backward. This time she tried to concentrate.

"Back. I've got it."

"Third is to the right and up."

"I think I have it."

"Now, each time you change the gears, you let the foot up on the clutch and press light on the gas, so it is even. Yes?"

"Yes. So that means your foot is already pressing down on the clutch when you start?"

"Yes. You got it. We try."

Lucy waited until the road behind her looked clear then she turned the wheel and tried to make the car go forward as she eased her left foot up and pressed down on the gas. The car crept forward.

"Yay! We're moving," she yelled, excited over her little victory.

"When you build a little speed, go to second."

"Back, right?"

"Right." Vittorio watched as they made their way down the narrow road, full of blind curves. "Maybe I should teach on a flat road," he said as they made a wide turn around a corner. Fortunately, there was no one coming up the other way.

"No, I can handle this," she said, grinding the gear into second.

Vittorio winced. "Slow on the gas. No force the stick. Just slide it in."

"Slide it in," Lucy repeated. "Guys are better at sliding things in than girls are."

Vittorio nodded. "Such things take practice."

"I bet," she said looking over at him. The car drifted over to the other lane. Vittorio grabbed the wheel. Another car passed them and honked.

"Watch the road, Lucia."

"I'm sorry," she said and took control again. "I've got it."

"Now third gear," he ordered, but she could tell he was a little agitated. "Slow. No push."

The car lurched forward and jerked as Lucy tried to get it into third gear.

"A little gas. A little clutch," Lucy said as she attempted all three things at once. She was determined to get it. Determined to master this silly, outdated way to drive.

Empowered, she straightened up and tried again, clutching, gassing, grinding gears as she snaked down the skinny road.

They drove along like this for about ten minutes. Lucy felt she had it, felt like this was as simple as learning the VI editor on her workstation. VI was one of the first text editors developed for a Unix-based station. It was riddled with strange shortcuts and abbreviations that only made sense to a techie. A person couldn't just type or delete without knowing all the right key strokes, but once you memorized the keys, or in this case, the right moves, you were home-free.

What's the big deal, she thought. Any moron can drive a stick.

Then in one masterful move, she took a bend in the

road a little too fast. She overcompensated by spinning the wheel and stepping on the clutch instead of the brake. She just missed a roadside fruit stand. Panicked, Lucy spun the wheel back, heading right for oncoming traffic. A guy in a white sedan swerved out of her way. Lucy totally lost it. Vittorio grabbed the wheel and headed straight into the nearest ditch.

The car stopped.

Vittorio both prayed and swore in accelerated Italian.

"Are you all right?" he asked, still speaking Italian.

"I'm fine," Lucy said. "A little dazed but in one piece."

She turned the car off and mindlessly slipped the key into her straw bag. Vittorio continued with his onslaught.

"Hey, we're all right. Calm down!" she yelled, trying to get him to stop.

But there was no calming him. After all, it's what Italians did best. They yelled, and fussed and gyrated their anger like parrots acting out a mating dance.

"Why did I ever think you could drive my car? What was I thinking! I must be crazy. Crazy! I'm a crazy man." He slapped his forehead. "We could have died and I would have let you kill us because I am insane!" He couldn't stop even when he got out of the car. Even when the guy from the other car walked over. Vittorio just kept foaming.

Lucy opened her car door and slid out, admittedly a little dazed. She slammed the door and studied the front tire caught in the ditch.

"I never did get the VI editor," she said out loud and kicked the tire.

When she looked up, the sun was in her eyes. She

put her hand up on her forehead to block it, but she still couldn't actually see. Vittorio and the guy she had forced off the road were talking. Actually, the guy was talking, Vittorio was waving his arms, yelling.

"Are you all right, miss?" an older male voice asked. He spoke Italian.

"Fine. Thanks," she answered in English. He was a sweet little guy, older, midseventies and completely toothless. Okay, maybe he had a few of his molars, but she couldn't quite tell from his smile.

Speaking in English, he said, "You want to sit down? I got a nice chair over there and some fresh lemonade." He pointed to the fruit stand—a bright blue truck with orange, yellow and green plastic crates surrounding it. Each crate was filled to the brim with fresh fruit. A wooden chair stood off to the side, covered by a cherry-striped umbrella. It looked so inviting and he was so sweet that she decided to take him up on his offer while the two men did their pissing thing.

"I'd like that," she told him and they walked back to his stand. "My name is Lucia. I'm from California."

"Ah, California! They got good fruit in California," he said.

"Yes," she mumbled. "Good fruit." It suddenly struck her, as they walked back together, after she had agreed about the good fruit in California, that she had told him her name was Lucia. And what was even more amazing, she had liked saying it.

"Here, sit, Lucia. It's cool under the umbrella."

After she drank down almost the entire glass of the absolute best lemonade she had ever tasted, and was feeling better, Vittorio and the other guy headed her way. She still couldn't see, not really, just outlines, but there was something about the way the other guy walked. Something that reminded her of…she couldn't even complete the thought. Didn't want to complete the thought. It was too silly. Too B-moviesque.

But still.

She stood up as they got closer. The light shifted to their backs with the curve in the road as they headed her way, waiting for a car to pass them, then another. She stood up and a knot centered itself in the pit of her stomach, the back of her neck tightened, her breathing became difficult.

She waited until the men were right in front of her, until she could be sure, until she could actually see without the sun blinding her view.

Then he spoke and with the first syllable she sat back down in her chair.

"Lucy? What the hell—? Are you all right, babe?" Seth asked, kneeling down to look into her eyes. "You're shaking."

"Uh-huh," was all she could say.

Vittorio's look at Lucy was so obviously confused that she honestly didn't know what to do next, so she introduced the man she was falling in love with to her fiancé.

"Vittorio, this is Seth, my fiancé. Seth, this is Vittorio…my friend." She held out her hands, one to each of them, palms up, as if she was going to start weighing out the possibilities of the two men. As if she was some kind of scale weighing their attributes. She dropped her hands to her sides.

The two men eyed each other, but neither made a move for a handshake. Silence.

Seth spoke first, "Yeah, whatever. So this dude tells me you were driving. Is he your teacher or something?"

"Or something," Lucy answered.

Seth picked up on her response in a heartbeat. "Wait a minute. You look different."

"I do?"

"Your clothes. Where'd you get those clothes?"

"When in Rome."

"Your hair. What goes here?"

"What are you doing here, Seth?"

"I thought this was what you wanted. You told me you wanted to get married here. In Italy."

Lucy remembered her pleading phone call. She never actually thought he would take her up on it.

"Umm, about that phone call—"

"It was your idea for me to fly out here. Not mine."

"This isn't the place, or the time—"

"I couldn't even find you at work, and you're not registered at the Santa Maria. The receptionist at Subito guessed you'd be up here. Taking cooking lessons, she said. Is there something going on I should know about?"

Before Lucy could say a word, before she could tell him that she had postponed the wedding, that she didn't love him anymore, that she wasn't sure about anything anymore, Vittorio said, "What could be going on? Cooking. That's it. Nothing more."

Seth looked at Vittorio as traffic sped by behind them, as day-shoppers stopped to buy fruit, as Lucy's heart absolutely shattered.

"Okay then. Let me help you get your car out of the ditch. It's the least I can do after my girl put it in there," Seth said to Vittorio.

"I can do it, thank you. You and *your girl* have better things to do than to help me. You have a wedding to fly home to."

"That's why I'm here," Seth said, turning to Lucy.

Vittorio's gaze rested on Lucy. She couldn't tell what he was thinking or feeling, she only knew she wanted him to stop this. To tell Seth that *he* loved her. That what he felt for her was more than he could ever hope for. That he had finally found his true love and he would not let her go.

But instead he said, "Ah, *Buona fortuna!*" and picked up a glass of lemonade and held it up in the air for a toast of sorts. "Let me be the first one to wish that you should be always happy together."

Then he drank it down. It was her glass. Her lemonade. And for that brief crazy moment, while she watched him swallow, she thought that, somehow, no matter what happened, they would always be connected. Always be a part of each other.

Or not.

He spat it out. "This is sour," he said out loud.

The little fruit-stand guy heard him and yelled back in perfect English. "It's not sour. Your taste is sour!" he yelled.

"My taste is perfect. This is sour!" And Vittorio spat on the ground.

So much for always being part of each other, Lucy thought.

AFTER she grabbed her new straw bag from the Alfa Romeo, and pulled Andrew out from under the front seat, Lucy walked over to Seth's rental.

She opened her own door on the automatic Ford Focus, hesitated and glanced back at Vittorio. He watched, motionless, from the side of the road.

She waved and yelled, "*Arrivederci*, Vittorio."

"*Arrivederci*, Lucia," he said, but she couldn't actually hear him because of the traffic. Disappointed and saddened by the whole mess, Lucy sat herself down in the front seat of the very American car, threw her bag on the back seat, and Andrew settled on her lap.

"I wasn't sure I would find you," Seth said as he turned the key in the ignition, put the car in Reverse, backed onto the road, then shoved it into Drive and drove away...just like that. Without thought. Without hesitation. Suddenly an automatic seemed like a kid's tricycle instead of a ten-speed, a Vespa instead of a Harley. It was all so easy now. So mindless. Like driving with blinders on. Like living with blinders on. She wanted to tell him how exciting it was to drive a real car, a car with a stick shift, but instead she simply nodded and smiled.

"Did he give you that?" Seth asked, quickly glancing over at her, then back at the road.

Lucy froze. Was there a hickey on her neck? Some telltale sign that Vittorio had kissed her? Could it be that she hadn't noticed it? Would she have to confess everything to Seth right here in the car, like in *Moonstruck* when Loretta gets confronted by her mother for her love-bite?

Lucy grabbed her neck, covered it with her hand and tried to remain calm, tried to think of something clever to say. She wasn't quite ready for the truth. Not yet. Not while they were driving. Not when Seth could run them off a cliff in his torment. Or worse, run her off the cliff while he stood on the side of the road laughing as she plunged to her death in a fiery crash down the side of the mountain. "It's a beauty mark. I usually keep it covered with makeup but when my boots were stolen—"

"Somebody stole your boots?"

"Yes, but he didn't really hurt me when he pushed me down. It was the rain—"

"Wait a minute. Somebody pushed you down in the rain and stole your boots? When did this happen? Did you report it?"

"Well, actually, no. Let me see if I can straighten this out. It all started because I didn't wear the bell on my toe and no, you won't understand that part. Actually, it really started when I woke up with the violent lesbian and she—"

"Excuse me, but did you just say you woke up with a lesbian?"

She could tell he was getting angry, really and truly angry. This was not good. She had to think of another way to put this. The road was pretty scary, and Seth wasn't really paying attention. "Perhaps you should slow down."

"I've got it under control. Now go back to the part about you and the lesbian," he said and lost it going around a turn. Lucy's stomach flipped a couple million times before he got the car back under control.

"It really has nothing to do with her. I couldn't get a room so Rosalyn—"

"Rosalyn's a lesbian? Huh! I never would have guessed."

"Well, not exactly...but, look, this is what happened."

Lucy decided she should just tell him the whole miserable story. Put it out there for him finally to know the truth. Her eyes welled up from guilt, or was it fear? She didn't know. At that precise moment, she couldn't be sure what she was feeling.

He reached over and took her hand. She wrapped her fingers around his and tried to feel an emotion.

Something that would tell her the spark might still be there, but all she felt was confusion. Total and absolute confusion. Vittorio had thrown her emotions into hysteria and now she didn't know what to do. What to say.

But Seth needed to know the truth. Whatever that might be.

She turned to him ready for the confession. Ready to strip her heart naked with whatever jumbled-up stuff that might pour out of her mouth when he said, "Babe, I've known there was something wrong between us for a long time, and I forgive you. You couldn't help yourself. If you and Rosalyn—"

"Rosalyn? You're forgiving me for sleeping with Rosalyn?"

"Yeah, whatever you two girls did, I forgive you."

He winked. He actually winked at her. She couldn't believe it. "Oh, so it's okay if I slept with a woman, but not a man, is that it?"

"Let's not fight."

"Are you out of your frigging mind?"

"What did I say?"

"Let me out of the car."

"You're not getting out of the car."

"Yes I am. Let me out."

He pulled over. She got out, slammed the door and paced. Andrew watched her out the window. Seth watched her out the window. She paced some more. Seth got out of the car. She looked at him.

"I'm sorry," he said. "I'm sorry for everything."

"I am too," she said. "I—"

And just as she was about to bare her soul, right there on the worst road in Italy, while traffic came within inches of them and their car, risking a total jealous rage by an otherwise logical, sweet man, Seth interrupted her, took in a deep breath and said, "Actually, the reason why I flew all the way out here is to tell you in person that I don't want to marry you."

"What?" Lucy said, hardly able to believe the words that had come out of his mouth.

"I'm really, truly sorry, but I'm just not ready to get married. It's not you. It's me. You're a wonderful girl, but, well, I just don't love you enough to spend the rest of my life with you."

"And just when were you planning on telling me this? As we said our wedding vows?"

"I was going to tell you last week, but then this business trip of yours came up and I thought you would call me and postpone the wedding. I thought maybe we could take a break or something, so I could figure things out, but instead you phoned and wanted me to fly here. Well, I knew then that I had to tell you the truth. In person."

"But you ordered a mai tai fountain."

"Yeah, well, I thought if I could just get into the whole wedding thing I might change my mind and want to go through with it. But it didn't work. I'm sorry. I feel like a jerk about this whole situation, but I simply can't marry you."

Lucy was both hurt and outraged. There she was, so totally confused over every aspect of life, and there was Seth, completely focused on what he had to do. Completely in charge of his emotions.

Logical.

Rational.

Able to state his feelings in a clear and precise way.

She wanted to throw him and his rational, logical behavior over the cliff, but she got into the car instead.

Seth got back in and they took off down the road again, together.

After a while, Seth said, "You haven't answered my question. Where'd you get that?"

Lucy still did not know what he was talking about and at that point, didn't care if there was a huge hickey on her neck. She actually hoped there was a big, fat purple hickey staring right over at him.

"It's none of your business," she snapped.

"Okay, but I think there's some kind of law about bringing an animal back to the States, some kind of quarantine thing."

Lucy at once realized that he had been asking about the cat all along. She stared at him for a moment, blinking, thinking about his totally structured life, her now totally unstructured life, their non-life together and said, "Andrew belongs to Rosalyn."

# 20

"WHAT HAPPENED to you?" Rosalyn said when Lucy opened the front door of Subito, and stood in the doorway for a minute trying to coax Andrew to come inside. He was busy smelling the base of a palm tree and wouldn't budge. "We couldn't get you on your cell."

"Let's take the events in order. First, you lied to me," Lucy said.

"I never lie," Rosalyn replied.

Lucy picked up Andrew and walked inside. He immediately jumped out of Lucy's grasp and up onto Rosalyn's desk. "Hey, lover, what are you doing here?" she cooed to an affectionate Andrew.

"He's here because your roomie threw us out."

"Laura's home? She's a week early," Rosalyn said while scratching Andrew under his chin.

"She wanted to surprise you." Lucy stood with her hands on her hips. Mad.

"Aw, how sweet."

"Instead, she surprised me. Why didn't you come back to your apartment?"

"It's not my apartment anymore. I moved out with my Russian hottie," Rosalyn said, dangling a string in front of Andrew's face. Andrew batted at it with his paw. "Besides, that thing with Laura is so over. It was fun for a while, but all we did was fight over clothes and stuff...and all that lavender. She really needs to pick a different color."

Lucy wanted to smack Rosalyn. Anger boiled up inside her. "Then why did you leave me there?"

"I couldn't get you a room, remember? However, since then, I suppose you found one," she said with a wicked little smirk.

"Why did you send my fiancé out to Vittorio's?"

"Seth's really too candy-sweet for you."

Okay, now Lucy wanted to rip her head off. "What gives you the right—"

"Poor boy was frantic. I had no choice but to squeal."

Could she just scream? Scream at the top of her lungs. Lucy ached to let her voice rip through the building. "There was a good reason why I was at Vittorio's."

"Whatever." Rosalyn shrugged.

Unconsciously, Lucy stroked Andrew and stared at Rosalyn. She wore large rimless glasses, had her hair piled up on top of her head all curly-like, her sweater was soft pink and ultra-tight with three-quarter sleeves and pink faux fur around the scooped collar, the skirt, short and a deep, rich pink with matching slip-on sandals.

This was the woman who had lied to her, who had forced her to sleep with a cat, who was responsible for most of her miseries, who had probably, purposely, booked Vittorio's flight and put *him* in the seat next to the window. Rosalyn knew everything about Vittorio, seemed to know everything about Lucy's very soul and was simply the coolest chick she had ever met.

"I bought you a swimsuit from Maria Lampo's,"

Lucy told her, gently laying the tiny package on the desk.

"You did? Wow! Thanks, Lucy." Rosalyn tore open the wrapping and picked up the suit. It was even smaller than Lucy had thought.

"I love red. It's perfect. Thanks. I see you did a little shopping for yourself, as well," Rosalyn said, giving Lucy the once-over.

"Yeah. What do you think?" Lucy took a step back so Rosalyn could get the full effect.

"It's a perfect look for you. Hot!"

Lucy actually giggled. Granted it was a minor giggle, but a giggle nonetheless. And with Rosalyn!

Lucy regained some composure and went back to petting Andrew.

Rosalyn asked, "I thought you were allergic to cats."

"I am. I was." She took a breath. "Laura threw *us* out."

"Oh, poor Andrew. I hope you're not hurt, sweetie."

"Andrew! Andrew is fine! I couldn't register at the Santa Maria because of him."

"I could have told you that. They don't allow pets. But I hope you and Seth like the honeymoon suite I got you guys at the Miramare. It's on the Santa *Lucia* waterfront. Appropriate, don't you think? Where is the little American tart?"

"I don't know where he is. The wedding's off. His idea. He's not ready, but I'm 'a wonderful girl.' Where is everybody?" Lucy glanced at her watch. She hadn't worn it in two days, but it was back on her wrist now. "It's not even six yet, or are they still out to lunch?"

"Are you okay?"

"I'm fine. Really."

"Well, don't let it get you down, Lucy. There's other

cuties out there...and one of them works right next door."

"I don't think that's going to work out, but I don't want to talk about it right now. Any word on the project?"

"You'll be happy to know that the chip is clean, and ready for tape-out. Isabella is here doing whatever you guys do to get it ready."

"The chip is clean? When did the systems come back online? Is Frank here?"

"Yeah, Frank brought everything up yesterday about an hour after he got in."

"What? Why didn't anybody call me?"

"I think I did, once, but I couldn't get through."

"My phone was dead, but you could have kept trying. Left a message. Done something!"

"Why?"

"Because I could have helped. I could have—"

"Screwed things up? Look, I'm sorry, but you're caught in that American corporate bullshit where no one has a life, and if they do, it's only in their own mind."

"That's a nasty thing to say."

"But true. Look, these people work to live, not live to work. They get the job done, but you can't force them to work according to your plan. It just won't fit. Not here."

Lucy didn't answer. What could she say? Rosalyn was right.

As she looked around the small lobby, she realized the vending machines were gone. "Did you send them back?"

"Not all of them. The snack machine is next to Frank's office. He wanted to keep it, but Giovanni tried a pizza-pocket at two in the morning and got food poisoning, so after he came back from the emergency room he called the vending company. They're coming to get it in the morning.''

Lucy stared at Rosalyn. She really didn't know what to say. The only thing Lucy knew to be true at that exact moment was that she still had a job to do. She had to get the chip back to the States for fabrication.

''So, have you told him yet?''

''Told who what?''

''Have you told Vittorio that you're in love with him?''

''Don't be ridiculous.''

''You're in love with Vittorio.''

''That's impossible. I barely know the man.''

''You don't have to know somebody to be in love with them, and you're in love with Vittorio.''

''That's crazy.''

''Look at you.''

''What about me?''

''Your hair's all pretty and free, you're wearing a skirt, a sexy shirt and Italian sandals. You're in love all right, but you just don't want to admit it.''

''Shut up,'' Lucy said.

''Whatever you say, but you're making a mistake.''

''Well, if I am, and I'm not, Vittorio doesn't...not that it would matter because—''

There was a loud moan from the back room. ''Shh,'' Rosalyn said. ''Did you hear that?''

''What?''

Another moan, only somebody called for help this time.

Rosalyn got up and said, ''It's Isabella.''

The two women ran through the lobby and through the offices until they found Isabella sitting on the floor.

"It's the baby. It's time. But it's too fast. The contractions are too hard," Isabella said, concern on her face, her hands supporting her round belly. She was shaking.

"When did they start?" Rosalyn asked.

"About five hours ago."

"Five hours!" Lucy repeated.

"Why did you wait so long? Why didn't you go to the hospital?" Rosalyn asked.

"I wanted to send the chip to B-Logic, but it's not working."

"Dennis phoned me. There's a problem with the firewall. I'll call an ambulance," Lucy said.

"No. I don't want an ambulance. I don't want my baby born in an ambulance. I'm okay. Just drive me. It's only a few kilometers."

"How far apart are the contractions?" Rosalyn asked.

"About ten minutes. We still have time."

"I'll get Vittorio. He can drive you," Lucy said, and left.

On her way out, she grabbed her straw bag off the desk in the lobby, and ran out the front door. There, sitting right in front of Subito, sat Vittorio's Alfa Romeo. Lucy remembered that she still had the key. Should she do it? Should she drive Isabella to the hospital?

She turned around and went back in the front door. Rosalyn and Isabella were just coming into the lobby.

"I'll drive you," Lucy said with absolute assurance in her voice.

No one questioned her as Isabella moaned with another contraction. She leaned against the two women, arms intertwined as they helped her walk to the tiny red sports car.

"Isn't this Vittorio's car?" Rosalyn asked.

"Yes," Lucy answered, smiling, dangling the key in front of her face.

"You're stealing his car?"

"It's an emergency. I'm borrowing it."

"Borrowing it? Vittorio doesn't let anyone drive his car. Not even his own mother."

"I drove it this afternoon. Don't worry. We'll be fine."

"You take good care of Isabella," Rosalyn said.

Isabella told Rosalyn, "Call my Mario. Tell him not to worry. I'm in safe hands, but tell him to get to the hospital. Now!"

Lucy eased Isabella into the car, then closed her door, calmly walked around, and got in on the driver's side. Isabella and Lucy locked hands for a moment.

Lucy said, "Let's go have a baby."

Without even thinking, Lucy stuck the key into the ignition, stepped on the clutch, put her foot on the gas and as smooth as cream, Lucy Mastronardo guided Vittorio's car out into traffic and drove away.

# 21

"BREATHE! Don't push yet. He's not here," Lucy warned Isabella.

"Like I have control over this?" Isabella yelled during another contraction.

Beautiful Isabella lay in an automatic bed at Cardarelli Hospital with her upper body propped up in what looked like a most uncomfortable position. Sweat beaded on Isabella's perfect face and neck, her hair swirled in tiny damp ringlets on her shoulders, and her stomach, covered in a thin hospital gown, looked massive. How could a human stomach actually get that big and not explode or something, Lucy thought.

"Breathe!" Lucy repeated as she held Isabella's hand and wiped her forehead with a damp cloth.

"Where is my Mario? How could it take him this long to get here? I want my Mario!" Isabella shouted.

"He's on his way. I promise."

"I want him now."

"Let's think about something else, here. I heard that if you take your mind off the pain, it won't seem so bad."

"Yeah? Where did you hear that? In a staff meeting?"

"Okay, I understand that women get mean when they're in labor. I can handle it. Go ahead. Dish it out if it makes you feel better."

"What will make me feel better is my hand inside Mario's instead of your scrawny little thing." She pushed Lucy's hand away. "I can't take this much longer! I knew it would be bad, but not like this. Nothing can prepare you for this. Take my advice. Don't ever have any kids. Oh, no, here we go again."

Isabella reached for Lucy's hand and held tight.

"Breathe. In. Out. It can only last a few minutes." Lucy tried to soothe her. Tried to get her through each contraction while they waited for Mario. While they waited for the baby.

Isabella yelled out her pain. Lucy joined in on the yelling. They sounded like two wolves howling at the moon. It made Isabella laugh. Right there during a contraction, Isabella was laughing.

When it was over she told Lucy, "You're pretty funny when you're not presenting charts and lists or putting up vending machines. You can be here for all my babies."

"Only if you're there for mine," Lucy said, but Isabella started yelling again. Lucy joined in again, an octave below, trying for some harmony. Despite the agonizing pain of it all, Isabella had a smile on her face. So did Lucy. They held on to each other and howled away.

That's when the contractions changed pace. They were almost on top of each other, one right after the other without any breathing room in between.

WHEN VITTORIO walked outside his restaurant to drive Isabella's husband to the hospital, his car was missing. At first he thought perhaps he had parked it out back, but when he went to check, it wasn't there, either. That's when he panicked.

There was only one other person who had the keys to his car, and she was a catastrophe behind the wheel. Good thing he kept a spare in his wallet or he would still be stranded on Statale 163.

Mario couldn't wait, couldn't catch an empty cab, and couldn't find anyone else to drive him, plus he was so nervous about Lucy driving his wife to the hospital that he thought for sure he would find them crushed in some kind of horrible accident, so he took off running.

Vittorio tried to keep up, but the man had wings on his feet. After a while, Vittorio gave up and went back to his restaurant to wait it out.

He figured that by now Lucy and Seth were back to getting married on Saturday, or perhaps, right there in *Napoli* that very night, but whatever was happening with the two of them, he really didn't want to see her again. Not so soon after their day together. Not when the glow would still be on her face.

It had been a lousy ride back from the coast, a lonely ride back, and for the first time in his life, he actually missed the smile of a woman, a particular woman. A woman who had gotten under his skin, just like the Frank Sinatra song, and as quickly as she had, she was gone.

Vittorio wasn't the type of man to care about one woman when there were so many to choose from, but this one was special. He couldn't figure it out, the why of it. He had been with many women in his life, probably too many, yet this one lingered. It was the way she had kissed him, almost as if it were her first time, and yet he knew that was impossible. Still, he knew women, and she was so new to all of it, to real passion, to real love, the way she looked into his eyes, the way her lips lingered on his. Oh, those kisses. Like honey.

He didn't know what to make of all these feelings. Didn't know what he would do now that she would be married to some other man. And what kind of man was that who couldn't even keep his car on the road? So he was an engineer. So what! Engineers were strange people. Too tight. Too many numbers churning in their heads. Not enough love. A big shot in America. So what!

Vittorio only knew one thing for sure. Lucy did not love this big shot. This American. No woman could kiss one man with so much passion and be in love with another.

He had to admit it, he was absolutely and totally in love with a woman he would never see again.

A NURSE came in to check on Isabella and Lucy got up from the tiny chair she had been sitting on so the woman could do her thing. The nurse checked and poked and looked at the fetal monitor.

Lucy was at once fascinated by the whole experience and scared. Really scared. There was something so awfully terrifying about waiting for a woman's bones to stretch out so that an eight-pound baby could somehow slip through an opening the size of a straw.

"It's time," the nurse said.

"What do you mean 'it's time?' My Mario isn't here yet. It can't be time." But as she said it, another contraction started, only this time Isabella let out a basement moan that sent a shiver through Lucy so deep she thought she could actually feel the pain.

The nurse pressed a button on the wall above the bed and three other nurses appeared in the doorway. Everything moved so fast, Lucy had no time to adjust to what was happening. They wheeled Isabella out the

door and down a hallway. And just as somebody
handed Lucy a green paper gown, Mario ran into the
hallway in time to help beautiful Isabella bring their
baby into the world.

# 22

ISABELLA'S perfect baby girl cooed and squeaked as it lay in her arms. Mario beamed with pride. He stood next to his wife, holding her hand, gazing at his new baby daughter, Trina Gabriella Santelli.

"She's beautiful," Lucy told the proud parents. "She looks just like her mom."

"Thank you, Lucy. You were wonderful. I don't think I could have stood that last hour without you."

"I'd yell with you anytime, Isabella. You were magnificent."

"We were all magnificent, especially little Trina. Look at that sweet face. Could there be another baby with such a face? She's perfect."

"Just like her mother," Mario said, bending over to kiss his wife.

Lucy took it as her cue to leave. She picked up her bag and approached Isabella for a farewell hug. Lucy really liked Isabella. She admired the control she had over her life, the decisions she had made. Isabella knew exactly what she needed to make herself happy.

Unfortunately for Lucy, she still had no idea what would make her happy. Really, truly happy.

"I'd better go," Lucy said taking Isabella's hand.

"Not before you hold Trina," Isabella commanded with an alluring smile.

"I'd love to." Lucy bent over and took Trina from Isabella's arms. The baby was warm and tightly bundled as she moved her little head, squeezed her eyes and spread tiny fingers.

Lucy was instantly charmed by her contented face. "Look at you, you sweet-pie, all warm and sleepy." Lucy instinctively rocked her, and stroked her silky cheek. Little Trina was a sweetheart, just like her mom. And she had that wonderful baby smell of powder and spring.

Isabella said, "By the way, not to spoil the moment or anything, but now that my brain has returned, the chip is clean and ready to be sent. I tried to encrypt it so I could send it to the fab, but couldn't do it. Something is wrong with the program." She slid down on the bed, trying to make herself more comfortable. Mario plumped her pillows.

Lucy tried to stay in the Trina-moment, but work issues spun her back to reality.

"Can't Frank fix it?"

"I don't know, but there's a backup tape of the streamed-out gds version on my desk. If nothing else works, you can take it with you on the plane tomorrow morning."

Lucy hadn't really thought about going back, all she really wanted to do was sit in a rocking chair somewhere and sing to Trina. Suddenly the thought of motherhood and raising children seemed like a pretty special endeavor. One that she truly wanted to be part of, but not with Seth.

She hadn't really had time to think about their breakup, think about the ironic turn of events. After all, there she was guilting herself over her bad-girl behavior, and there he was eager to break the whole thing off because he just wasn't ready. Did Seth know something about love that she didn't? Did he instinctively know that what they had wasn't actually love, and that's why he'd broken it off?

Real love was written all over Mario's face when he looked at his wife and his new baby girl, and all over Isabella as she'd yelled out each contraction to bring Trina into the world. That's what Lucy wanted to know. To feel. She wasn't ever going to marry someone just because it was right for her career, or because of a plan. Next time she got engaged it would be to someone she truly loved and who loved her. If there ever was a "next time."

She held little Trina for one more moment, then reluctantly handed her back to her mom and said her goodbyes.

THE DRIVE BACK to the restaurant was exhilarating to say the least. She merged with all the other cars without so much as a hiccup. It was as if she had been driving a stick shift all her life. She even took the time to hang out the window and yell at another driver for cutting her off when the policewoman standing in the center of the street directed her to go.

"Are you nuts? Can't you see she told me to go and not you!"

The man yelled back at her, but she couldn't really hear him, just as he probably couldn't hear her, but it felt amazing to shout at the top of her lungs on a crowded street in *Napoli* where no one cared.

The parking space was still there when she pulled up in front of La Bella Note, and she slipped into it as though she had done it a million times before. Lucy continued to impress herself.

As she entered the restaurant, a tinge of apprehension settled in her now totally empty stomach. She wanted to see Vittorio even though she wasn't too sure what she should say. *Thanks for the driving lesson, thanks for taking me to Positano, thanks for cooking for me, and by the way, thanks for telling Seth you loved me and couldn't let me go.*

Yeah. Right.

She pondered those thoughts as she looked around the crowded restaurant, trying to find Vittorio or a familiar face. She spotted Rosalyn sitting at a table, way in the back. Not the face she particularly wanted to see, but at least she would have the key to Subito. She would simply pick up the key, get the tape and leave. She'd send Vittorio an e-mail...if he even had e-mail.

As Lucy got closer to the table, she realized that her ex-fiancé sat almost in the lap of that other bad girl, Rosalyn.

Well, she thought, that didn't take long.

Lucy felt actual jealousy for a moment, but then thought better of it because, in the scheme of her messed-up life, this was perhaps the greatest thing that could ever happen.

She marched to the back of the restaurant, courage shining on her face.

"Seth," she said as she approached the table. "I just want to say that I understand and I'm—"

But Seth was a little green in the jowls.

Lucy knelt down next to him so they were eye level. "Are you all right, Seth?" she asked him. But he could only look at her with vapid eyes.

Rosalyn said, "I don't know what happened. We were having such a good time and suddenly the poor baby got sick."

"What did you feed him?" Lucy asked as she felt Seth's clammy forehead.

"The same thing I ate. Pasta with garlic and butter sauce and a couple slices of garlic bread."

"He's allergic to garlic. Makes him vomit and shake, and—"

"Why didn't he tell me? Vittorio made it extra spicy just for him."

"Seth," Lucy said. "How do you feel?" He looked down at her and smiled a dumb-ass grin. Something else was wrong with him. "How much wine did he drink?"

"A lot, why? Is he allergic to wine, too?"

"Only red wine."

"Well, that explains it. He drank a whole bottle of Chianti. Will he explode or something?" Rosalyn jumped out of her chair, preparing for the worst.

"Maybe. He's never eaten so many bad things in one meal."

Rosalyn stared at her with a silly grin. "What should we do?"

"I don't know. He's never done this before."

"I want to go home," Seth mumbled. He got up from his chair, knocking it over. An older couple at the next table glanced at him with disgust on their faces.

Lucy tried to appease them as she stood up. "It's all right. He's not Italian. Can't hold his garlic," she whispered as if it was a shared secret. They nodded, smiled, and went on with their meal.

Seth moved in closer, got right in her face and said, "Who are you and what did you do with Lucy? Are you some kind of alien who's taken over her body? Some kind of pod-woman? You don't dress like her, or look like her. You may sound like Lucy, but you're not

Lucy. Not really. I know Lucy very well and you are definitely not her." He threw his white napkin on the table in some kind of defiant act.

He was genuinely angry. Livid, even. Seth Ingvar could get mad, after all.

"I'm sorry, Seth. Really I am."

"You're sorry! I'm sorry we ever got together in the first place." He paused, looked around and said, "What in-love person goes to Italy a week before their wedding and expects everything to be fine? No one, that's who." He paused again. Swallowed a few times and said, "I think I'm going to be sick."

Vittorio appeared out of nowhere, wrapped his arm around Seth's shoulder and escorted him to the toilets in the back of the restaurant.

Rosalyn said, "Now that it's over between you and Seth, can I have him? I kind of like the little darlin'. He's so cuddly."

"Have you always been like this, or is this just a phase you're going through?"

"No, I've pretty much always been this way."

They stared at each other, Rosalyn smiling, Lucy scowling. The nerve of this girl, Lucy thought. I'm not even out of the room yet and she's making a play for my boyfriend, fiancé or whatever he was now that they weren't getting married anymore.

"Just promise me one thing," Lucy said.

"I'm not too good at promises."

Lucy stepped in closer and got that vending-machine-rage look on her face. Rosalyn backed off. "Okay, so I'll keep this promise."

"Whatever you do, don't ever feed him garlic and red wine again."

They stared at each other, then Lucy smiled.

Rosalyn smiled.

The two women laughed out loud, and a week's worth of tension and animosity vanished in a heartbeat.

Vittorio walked out of the back with Seth. He looked a little better, the green was gone. Vittorio said something to Seth and left. Rosalyn followed, leaving Lucy and Seth alone in the back of a noisy, crowded Italian restaurant. She approached Seth, and as she did she could tell by the look on his face that he already knew exactly what she was about to say.

"I should never have let you go, right?" he asked.

"Yes," she answered, clearheaded and calm. She had to tell him without emotion.

"I loved you. We had our whole lives planned out, but I knew it was over as soon as you got on that plane. It just took me a few days to realize it. Then when I saw you on the side of the road, with Vittorio...I wanted the split to come from me. Not from you."

"I'm sorry, Seth, but I don't want my life planned like some time-management course. That's fine for you, but not for me, not anymore."

"Does he love you?"

"I don't know."

It was the first time Lucy had actually thought about Vittorio's love. Could he love her? Could a man like him love just one woman? Or would she end up like some sappy country-and-western song, with her man always foolin' 'round?

She didn't know the answer to that question.

"Do you love him?"

"I don't know that, either. I don't know what I feel, I only know I can't marry you. I can't live my life for somebody else. It has to be for me, or I can't breathe."

He kissed her on the cheek, gave her a really tight hug and let her go. "If I wasn't sick and drunk I'd probably throw a chair, but I think I'll just sit here and drink a soda water. This Pellegrino stuff is pretty good."

Rosalyn appeared, her timing impeccable. "Allow me," she said pouring him the glass of water.

There was a small part of Lucy that wanted to reach out for him, tell him it was all a mistake. It would be so easy just to go home with him and get married. Her father would be happy, but then she wasn't alive to live her father's life. She was meant to live her own life, no matter how weird or strange it might seem.

Vittorio walked up behind her.

"Lucia, you want to go for a walk? I think we can talk better outside," he said taking her hand.

His touch sent her spinning.

Was this what love felt like? Was he what love looked like?

"Yes," she said. "We should talk."

# 23

WHEN THEY were out in the garden, he turned to Lucy and kissed her. She kissed him back, feeling the power of this majorly important kiss. One of those tell-all kind of moments when the guy is supposed to get it. Get that he's in love with you.

He pulled away and said, "Lucia, I thought you were married. Gone."

"I thought you didn't care. The way you acted out on the road today. You let me go so easily."

"But how could I act? He is your fiancé. I am just your lover."

"He *was* my fiancé."

"What do you mean?"

"He broke it off, the relationship, the wedding, everything. He knew I—" but she couldn't finish the sentence. Couldn't tell him what was swirling abound in her heart.

"Will you go home tomorrow?"

"Yes, I have to take a tape back to B-Logic. It's what I came here for. What they pay me for. I have to go."

He let her go and walked away.

"How did you get back here today? I had your keys," she said, wanting to change the subject for a moment. "I'm sorry if I caused you any problems."

"This was not a problem. I keep the extra key in my

wallet. My problem is that I want you to stay. Send this tape. Stay here with me."

She couldn't believe it. The cad was telling her exactly what she wanted to hear.

"Come with me," she countered without thinking. "You can open that restaurant in San Francisco just like you wanted. I can help you."

"But I am not ready for this. I don't have the money."

"The money will come. It always does. I have some money saved. I can be your partner. Isn't this what you want?"

"Yes, but it is too soon. You stay here with me, in my house, in my bed."

"Are you asking me to marry you?"

He got a puzzled look on his face.

"Lucia, I am asking you to live in my house. I will take care of you. You will not have to work. You stay home. My house is beautiful, no? We will have fun together, just like we did today."

She was stunned. Vittorio was actually asking her to be his stay-at-home mistress.

"And where would you live?"

"Ah, I have my restaurant to run, and my mamma, she—"

"Don't say another word. As tempting as your offer may sound, I have a life back in the States. A life with a career that I've worked hard for and a promotion I deserve. I can't give it up. Not now, and definitely not to be your lover."

"But I cannot give you any more than that. I am not ready to leave here."

"And I'm not ready to leave the Valley, not yet anyway. You've taught me a lot, Vittorio, and one of those lessons is to live my life for me. You're asking me to live it for you. I can't do that." She took his hand, gave him the key to his Alfa Romeo and looked into his eyes. "Thanks," she said, "thanks for the ride of a lifetime."

"Lucia," he said, but she turned and walked away.

He called after her a couple times, but she just kept walking.

LUCY STOPPED at Subito, picked up the mag tape from Isabella's desk, picked up her laptop from Frank's desk, wrote a quick thank-you note to the elusive Frank, and left.

She grabbed a cab out front. It was the same NASCAR racer who'd picked her up that very first day.

"To the airport, please, but first, do you know where I can pick up a pound of prosciutto?" she asked and strapped herself in, tight.

"Sure, *signorina*. The best," he said as he squealed away from the curb.

This time she was ready for his speed ride and actually enjoyed the craziness of it all, laughing when he drove over curbs or cut off busses. She thought perhaps she was either insane or *Napoli* had finally gotten to her.

He pulled up in front of a small deli on the outskirts of town. A sign hung out front. It said Donico's. Lucy couldn't believe it. It couldn't be the same Donico.

As it turned out, Donico was a common enough name in Naples, and the little white-haired man who worked inside didn't actually know her mother, but said that a cousin of a cousin of an uncle on his mother's side might remember her. And in that case, he sold Lucy two pounds of prosciutto for the price of one. Her mother would be thrilled over the good deal on the salty ham.

SHE SPENT the rest of the night trying to sleep across two uncomfortable black chairs in the United terminal at the airport in Naples. All night long she kept thinking that Seth would show up to beg her to take him back and what she would say. Or Vittorio would sit down next to her with a ticket in his hand for San Francisco. She tormented herself with various scenarios featuring Vittorio, then Seth, then Vittorio, crying over the whole miserable mess. She blamed herself for ever having hitched a ride with Vittorio in the first place. None of this would have happened if she had only learned how to drive a stick shift when she was sixteen.

She fretted and fussed until finally, somewhere right before dawn her brain gave up the battle and she fell into a deep, cleansing sleep.

When morning came, she freshened up in the ladies' room, bought an espresso and a bottle of water, ate a chocolate biscotti and walked back to the terminal to wait for her plane to board.

While she sat waiting for the voice to come over the loudspeaker and tell her what rows were boarding, she decided she and Seth had done the right thing and she wouldn't cry about it anymore.

So, she didn't.

At nine-thirty on Friday morning her plane took off from Capodichino Airport, eight kilometers from the center of Naples.

She found her seat right next to the window. This time she double-checked just to be sure. It was a crowded flight and she didn't want any mistakes.

When breakfast arrived, a dry muffin and an omelette, she couldn't eat it. She tried, and it wasn't terrible, but all she could think of was the luscious cuisine of *Italia*, and the smell of this tiny omelette made her stomach swirl.

"Take this away," she told the female attendant. "I'd rather eat my shoe." But the attendant didn't get it.

When the plane landed in San Francisco, she had no problem getting through customs with just one straw bag and a makeup case, so she was back in her car in no time.

Drained and tired, she showed up at work right around three o'clock on Friday afternoon.

Everything looked the same: same blue walls, same blue cubes, and the same set of problems. She could hear someone standing in the aisle next to her cube complaining about not being able to get an LVS license, complaining about support.

Just complaining.

Lucy put her bag down on her desk and called I.T. A male voice said, "Can I help you?"

"Yes," Lucy answered. "I need a tape loaded onto the system right away."

"Is this a work stoppage?"

"Yes," she said. "It's gds data. I have to transfer it to fab today."

"I'll send somebody over."

"Thanks," she said into the phone.

She walked over to Vern's cubicle. He was a co-worker she had tried to get to go to Italy instead of going herself. She had to smile thinking that she would be getting married tomorrow if it wasn't for his fear of flying. Vern sat with his back to her, his headphones on, his head bobbing to his own music. He had one of those monitor mirror things stuck up on the corner of his monitor so he could see who walked in.

He turned, smiling. "Wow! You look different."

She blushed. "In a good way, I hope."

"Yeah. Great. How was Italy?" he asked.

"Hectic," she said.

"Same as here?"

"Not quite. They have a little different work ethic."

"Probably better, huh?"

Lucy had never had time to think about it, but she said, "Yeah. Totally."

"Congratulations on your promotion."

"What are you talking about?"

"Your promotion. Hello, Miss Jet Lag. Your promotion to director of project managers. How soon they forget!"

Lucy was stunned. Had he heard a rumor? Was he playing a dirty trick on her? "What do you mean?"

"I bet they didn't bother to tell you. You know how management is around here. They lay on the work, stick in a promotion and expect everyone to keep on truckin'. Dennis sent out a company-wide e-mail last Wednesday. Didn't you get it?"

Her thoughts spun around, trying to grasp what he was saying.

"I got the promotion? But Dennis said—"

"Not just a promotion, but an upper-management-type promotion. You should read your e-mail once in awhile."

"I didn't get a chance...things got a little out of hand and—" Lucy stopped herself. She wasn't about to explain everything to Vern. He wouldn't understand.

"Well, go read," he said.

Lucy started to walk away, then remembered why

she had walked over to his cubicle in the first place. "I.T. is loading the S9293 onto the system. When it comes up, would you please encrypt it and send it off to fab. It's all set up for you."

"No problem," he said and slipped his earphones over his ears and turned back to the layout on his screen.

When Lucy got back to her cubicle, she logged on and brought up her e-mail. She had one hundred and forty-two e-mails.

A record.

At first she couldn't find it, then she reorganized everything alphabetically and there it was, a corporate message from Dennis Chartrand.

From: "Dennis" (dc@blogic.com)
To: ALL
Subject: Promotion—Lucy Mastronardo
  Please join me in congratulating Lucy Mastronardo in her promotion to Director of Program Managers.
  Lucy has been with the company for the past six years and during that time has been instrumental in our continued success. She has been directly responsible for the timely completion of countless projects which have led to highly profitable industry wins.
  Her latest achievement is the S9293 which she handled with complete professionalism and taped out two weeks early.
  Congratulations, Lucy, on a job well done.
                                        Dennis Chartrand
                                        CEO B-Logic

"Two weeks early!" Lucy said out loud.

She couldn't believe she had gone through all that and no one had told her the real tape-out date! They were scum. Upper management was absolute scum.

Wait a minute, she thought. She *was* upper management and she certainly wasn't scum. She would have to make some changes. This lying about the tape-out date would have to stop.

But it did make everyone work harder, work faster. Were all those bean counters right?

"Oh my God," she said as she slid down in her ergonomic chair. She hadn't been in her new position for five minutes and she was already agreeing with them.

This was a serious problem.

Her phone rang.

She picked up. "This is Lucy."

"Good, you're home."

"How did you know?"

"A mother knows these things."

"But—"

"You gave me your itinerary."

"Oh," Lucy said, and took a swig of her bottled water. It was warm from being in her straw bag for the last fourteen hours.

"Things have changed. You better come home right away," her mother told her.

Lucy immediately thought the worst. "Why? What's wrong?"

"Nothing's wrong. Why should anything be wrong? I'm excited, that's all!" she squealed.

Her mother never squealed. "What's going on, Mom? Why the excitement?" Lucy asked.

"Can't a mother be excited without her daughter thinking the worst?"

"Mom, what are we talking about?"

"Your father and me wanted to tell you in person. I wasn't too sure I could do it until I tried it on. But I let it out a little in the bust, I always did have a big bust-line you know, and I hemmed it a couple inches. Now, it's perfect!"

Lucy was completely confused. "Wait a minute. Tried what on? Hemmed what a couple inches?"

"Your wedding dress. Why don't you listen when I talk? Your dress, it fits perfect. Like I picked it out for myself. I don't know what you were thinking. Too much dress for you. I look just like Sophia Loren, only I got a bigger bustline."

"I think I'm missing something here. Why are you trying on my wedding dress?" Silence. "Mom?"

"Your dad and me are getting married all over again."

Lucy sat up straight. "What? How? When?"

"Tomorrow. When else? Me and your father are gonna renew our vows. We're in love all over again. Just like teenagers. And he's taking me to Positano for the honeymoon. We never got one in the beginning 'cause he was working, but now he's taking the time off. Six weeks. What do you think of that, huh?"

Lucy was completely blown away.

"I'll be right there. Don't move."

She hung up, grabbed her straw bag and left.

"You look beautiful," Lucy told her mom as they stood in the back of Saint Christopher's waiting for the organist to give them their cue.

"I know," her mom said, a sly smile on her face.

They hugged. Her mom smelled wonderful, like a spring garden filled with...some kind of flower.

Lucy watched as her dad took her mother's arm, proud, happy and dapper in his black rented tux. Her mom was completely glowing as she stood by his side.

Funny, Lucy thought. Love was all around me and I never even noticed.

The "Wedding March" began, and Lucy walked down the aisle in front of her parents. It all seemed surreal. Almost as if she were caught in one of her dreams. She wished that somehow it *was* one of her crazy dreams and in reality Vittorio was waiting for her in the front of the church. He'd be wearing a fabulous Armani tux that fit him perfectly and she'd be in a simple Vera Wang. When they finally met in front of the altar, he'd take her hand and....

"We are gathered here today to—"

And so it began. Her parents really were getting married all over again and using her wedding to do it. She had to struggle to hold back the tears. Her mom looked beautiful, just like Sophia Loren. Lucy'd never seen her so happy. And when she took her dad's hand, Lucy could see it in their eyes. The same look that Mario and Isabella had for each other.

That incredible look of love.

"It's perfect," Lucy said to the car dealer. "I'll take it."

"I'll have finance draw up the contract. It'll just be a few minutes."

Lucy stood in front of a brand-new, turquoise Alfa Romeo Spider. *Her* brand-new, turquoise Alfa Romeo Spider.

It was Monday morning. A work day. But she didn't quite make it all the way to B-Logic. Didn't quite make it to see if everything had gone well with the chip. She'd had something to do first. Something she'd been desperate to do ever since she'd driven down Statale 163. Trade in the roomy, easy-to-drive, practical Toyota for a compact, hard-to-drive, impractical Alfa Romeo.

She eased herself into the driver's seat and closed her eyes, one hand resting on the steering wheel and the other on the stick. It felt right, the way it was supposed to be.

She knew the difference now, about cars and love and dangerous roads. Knew what was important about life, her life and her career.

And it felt great!

She took in a deep breath, filling her lungs with the sweetness of serenity.

Super great, she thought.

In that moment, Lucy decided that today was a hooky day and she couldn't wait to drive...anywhere.

# Epilogue

*Three months later...*

"BUT I WANT the car I ordered," Vittorio told the Alamo attendant behind the car-rental counter.

"I'm sorry, sir, but we don't have any stick shifts available, only automatics."

Lucy watched from a distance as Vittorio's anger swelled. His hair was a little longer now, with that messy look, but he still had his sideburns. He had gotten even more exciting to look at since they had been apart, or was that because she hadn't been able to get his touch, or his kisses out of her mind?

"This is crazy. What kind of a man drives an automatic? This is not an automobile. It is a kid's toy. I cannot drive a kid's toy."

Lucy had arrived at SFO early, two hours early. She was so excited she couldn't sleep. "Vittorio will arrive on flight 642, at 10:30 a.m. on Saturday. This Saturday," Rosalyn's e-mail had said, and Lucy had been preparing for it ever since, but she still wasn't quite sure what she would say or how she would act.

She and Vittorio hadn't actually spoken since the night she'd left, not really. She had only heard about him through Rosalyn and the media, but now, there he stood. The chef who had come to San Francisco to open his restaurant. The chef who had been on countless cooking shows and had become as popular as Emeril and Wolfgang Puck.

This chef...this man she loved with all her heart.

Her toes itched.

"I can drive you," she said, standing behind him, once again caught up in the ambiance that was Vittorio.

He turned at the sound of her voice, "*Perdona*, but have we met?" he asked with a mischievous grin.

"Lucia Mastronardo," she answered, extending her hand.

"Ah, Lucia. I am Vittorio Bandini." He took her hand in his. "Thank you, but I can drive myself."

"Nobody with a brain wants to drive a car in San Francisco," she said, still holding his hand.

"Ah, and what does this make you?"

"No brains. No brains at all. Please, let me drive—"

But she didn't finish her sentence. He encircled her in his arms and kissed her...and kissed her...and kissed her some more, until she could barely stand, until she could barely breathe.

Finally, he pulled back. Her head rested on his shoulder as she tried to regain some degree of composure, but it was completely impossible.

The attendant behind the counter cleared his throat, pulled on his collar and said, "So, I guess you won't be needing the car then."

"Thank you. No," Vittorio answered "I think it is better to take her. Yes?"

"Yes, better to take me," Lucy echoed. "I have a stick shift."

"Ah, a stick shift. Now this is an automobile," he said, and kissed her again, and again, and...well, he had to stop sometime.

Didn't he?

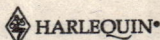

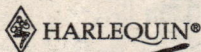